Cherish Him

Honey Bay, Volume 2

Steve Milton

Published by Steve Milton, 2022.

This is a work of fiction. Similarities to real people, places, or events are entirely coincidental.

CHERISH HIM

First edition. October 31, 2022.

Copyright © 2022 Steve Milton.

ISBN: 979-8215507926

Written by Steve Milton.

Table of Contents

1 1
2 11
3 19
4 30
5 46
6 59
7 72
8 82
9 90
10 96
11 109
12 120
13 126
14 140
15 145

1

Ted

"Do you also piss in sinks?" I strained my voice at whoever was inside the limo that had just parked on my precious lawn. "Did anybody ever teach you proper behavior?"

I banged my hand just a little too hard on the living room window. It hurt. The limo still didn't move off my lawn. In fact, it pulled a little bit closer to my door, just driving on my lawn. Some people truly had no sense of propriety.

I got dressed. I marched right outside. I tapped on the driver's window. It was tinted too dark to see inside, but I shouted loudly enough for whoever was inside to hear.

"The street is for parking. My lawn, on the other hand, is for—" I paused. What was my lawn for? "My lawn is for lawning!" I raised my arms in exasperation. "Parking. Lawning. Do you understand the distinction between the two?"

No answer. Maybe there weren't even humans inside, only vulgar monsters who had descended upon Earth only to park upon unsuspecting people's lawns.

"Is tearing up someone's lawn with your thirty-two-foot land yacht the accepted custom on whatever planet you're from?"

I strained my face up against the window's dark tint.

The limo's back door opened. A tower of upstyled hair peeked out from behind the door. A man — young, cocky, in a branded sweatsuit on a balmy Florida morning — stepped out of the limo and right onto my lawn.

He smirked at me. "You were the naked dude yelling from the house window?"

My face flushed red. I had indeed neglected to cover up when responding to the limo-on-lawn situation.

"Formerly nude dude yelling from the house window," I corrected, then did a half-second glance down to make sure it was true. "And it's my house window. It's my lawn. Anyway, formerly nude."

"Alright, Florida Man." He looked me over. "Formerly nude Florida Man."

"And you are?" I looked him up and down. With his haircut, his hoodie, and his cocky grin, he looked like he made his living posting on Instagram.

"I'm your new tenant." He glanced over at my house.

As if I'd even allowed that.

"My new tenant of what?" I squinted at him.

"Your new tenant of the Airbnb apartment. That you listed online? On Airbnb? The website?" He said it like a question.

Maybe I could pretend to have never heard of Airbnb. Maybe I could pretend that there was a recent re-addressing initiative and he was actually at the wrong house.

"You want to stay at my house?" I'd avoid it if there was any way. "There's no vacancy."

"My manager already arranged it for me." He showed me a confirmation email on the screen of his phone. He looked up and down the street, as if he was expecting to see someone he knew.

"Ah. That reservation." I sighed audibly. I had to own up to it. I'd already received the first batch of money from Airbnb for a three-month rental. My music store wasn't exactly a profit center of anything.

I needed the money. I just didn't need this guy.

He took off his sunglasses. He looked at me as if I should've been grateful to catch a glimpse of his face. "I'm Dante. Dante Huxley. You've probably heard of me." He grinned.

"I haven't." I looked at him blankly. "I'm Ted Baker. I own a music store. My cultural knowledge is mostly music based."

He shook his shoulders a little, like he was dancing, or a horse trying to shake free of its harness. "My band? Inferno? I'm sure you've heard of it."

"I've heard of it." That was the kindest thing I could say about Inferno. Just the typical cookie-cutter fluffy boy band. A couple of guys singing forgettable songs with forgettable lyrics. "Can't say I'm a fan."

I'd heard of Inferno. I certainly didn't condone it.

"Yeah?" Dante looked surprised. "If you own a music store, Inferno probably paid for your house." Dante smiled a huge, proud smile. He looked over my house top to bottom, like he was about to repossess it from me.

"What?" I took a step back, enough to notice his tight young body peeking out from under his muscle shirt. That shirt didn't really cover much of anything.

"Inferno albums sell like hotcakes, man. Probably paid for your house." Dante's eyes were a verdant green, the color of fresh guava. All that male beauty, strictly for the enjoyment of women. What a waste.

No boy band had ever paid me anything. I'd bought the house back before Honey Bay had become fashionable. "You think you paid for my house?" I shook my head.

"Inferno is at the top of the music charts. The music always sells well." Dante squinted as he stared at me, then at the house. "I'm just trying to tell you that if you're in the music business, then you'd better know Inferno. Inferno's music sells really well."

"I don't consider that sort of thing to be music." I smiled at him, kindly, the way the Pope would have smiled at a wayward pilgrim. I was being generous. I wasn't lashing out. "But as per Florida law, I don't discriminate against people who make shitty bubblegum pop. So yes, I will rent the place to you."

Dante pointed one silver-ringed finger at his limo. The trunk popped open. The driver jumped out and started unloading suitcases.

All this, on my lawn. No one cared. Not even an apology.

"I guess just put them there." Dante nodded to the driver and pointed at the front door of my house.

Weighed down like a mule, the driver tugged some suitcases, and a guitar, to my front door. No regard at all for what the luggage wheels were doing to my lawn, nor the way he carelessly kicked open the cat gate in front of the house proper.

"Let's discuss some basic things. Some ground rules." I cleared my throat. "This, you might not know, because you might never have seen one in New York City, is called a lawn." I gestured at its wide expanse. "I pay a hundred dollars a week for this lawn to be cut, styled, and conditioned."

"You must be doing pretty well." Dante nodded. "Those Inferno CDs must be selling at your store."

I withheld my latent rage and only politely shook my head. "My financial situation is irrelevant. I just have a sense — an understanding — of the importance of — the proper..." I sighed. It was no use. It was like singing opera to a pig. I'd just treat him as a tenant and not try to teach him about the finer things. "Let me show you inside."

"Cool. I love the bumfuck-nowhere small-town vibe here." Dante said it like it was nothing. Like after insulting my house and my livelihood, he could just insult my hometown. Nose in the air, looked like a drug-sniffing cocker spaniel. "The ocean air smells just like I remember. I used to do summer camp in Honey Bay when I was a kid. That's how I know it. It still makes me happy."

At least Dante was happy. At least somebody was happy. His driver stood next to the stack of suitcases and stared at Dante blankly. I led Dante over to the cat gate.

"And do you see this gate?" I tapped on the waist-high gate that separated the house proper from the lawn.

"Yeah." Dante nodded, then tapped on the fence just as I'd done. Dante see, Dante do. His long, thin fingers were downright simian.

"You have to make sure this gate is always closed." I opened the house's front door and pointed at Duchess. At the foot of the stairs, she was assessing the situation and licking her paws. "The gate has to stay closed so my cat, Duchess, won't run away."

"Her? Run away?" Dante glanced at Duchess and snickered. "I don't think she's gonna run anywhere. Roll away, maybe."

"What?" I distracted myself from anger by fishing around in my pocket for the key I'd saved for the tenant. "Duchess is big-boned."

Dante pointed at her again, rudely. "Big-boned? She looks like a ham." He chuckled again.

"I'm quite proud of how well I've fed her since adopting her from the shelter—" I shut up and gritted my teeth. It was no use trying to reason with someone like that. I'd give him his key and minimize all future contact.

"Here's the key. It opens the house and also opens your apartment, which is up the stairway and to the left." I handed him the key, complete with a Deep Down Music keychain. Maybe he'd stop by my store and learn about real music.

"Alright, man." Dante nodded and tossed the key in the pocket. He didn't even bother looking at the keychain. That was how much regard he had for real music.

He waved to his chauffeur, who without even greeting me, was wheeling suitcases up to the front door. "Your apartment is upstairs, not downstairs, by the way." I wanted to make it clear, just in case they were expecting me to carry those bags upstairs. This wasn't a hotel, and I was certainly nobody's bellboy.

"Yeah, cool." Dante nodded. Maybe he was planning on leaving his suitcases downstairs. Maybe there was a third dude, still hiding in the limo, for carrying the bags upstairs.

"Alright, rules of the house." I cleared my throat. "No parties, no guests, no smoking, no ganja." I pointed directly in his face.

He only shook his head.

I gestured to the rest of the house. "You can use any part of the house you want, including the kitchen, but I'm not your maid, so clean up after yourself. Feel free to use the patio and grill outside. There's charcoal in the outdoor closet. Alright?"

"Cool." Dante nodded.

The rules were *cool*, apparently.

"And just to remind you again: keep that outside gate closed."

"Got it!" Dante made an *ok* gesture with his thumb and forefinger. I didn't even bother to tell him how rude that was in Italy.

"Welcome to Honey Bay. I hope you enjoy your stay." I forced myself to shake his hand. "I've got to get to my music store. My contact info is in my Airbnb profile. Nice doing business with you."

I ran out the door. I hoped I'd never see him again. The fifteen hundred a month would just show up in my bank account. The money, I definitely didn't mind seeing.

As I walked out to my car, Dante's chauffeur was lugging suitcases upstairs. I averted my eyes to avoid looking at the limo still parked on my lawn.

I pulled up to Deep Down Music at exactly ten A.M. Angelica had already opened the store and stood smiling next to the cash register. She waved at me the same way she did every morning. No matter what little jerks passed through my life, Angelica was at least my friend. Had been for ages. Or at least since kindergarten.

"Guess what, Ted!" Angelica smiled and held V signs up next to her face. "Guess what, guess what! Big news of the town! Guess what it is!"

I sighed as I unlocked my office behind the front counter. "I don't know, Angelica. What's the big news? Andy Silver told a funny joke? Penny's Pancakes passed a health inspection? You've quit smoking marijuana?"

"No, silly!" Angelica rolled her eyes, the same way she did when customers asked if she was my girlfriend. "There's a celebrity in town!"

"Finally, I get the recognition I deserve." I nodded wearily. "It took you too long to realize it."

"Not you, Ted." Angelica clicked her tongue. "Dante Huxley! From Inferno! He's supposed to be here in Honey Bay!"

"Oh yeah?" I shook my head. It wasn't that I didn't believe it. It was more like I didn't want to deal with it. That insouciant little bubblegum-pop guitar-strummer wasn't just in my town. He was in my very house. Pulling his useless suitcases up my precious hardwood-floored stairs. "For real now, Angelica?"

"Deadass for reals!" Angelica made the V-signs next to her face again.

"Angelica, you're thirty-two years old."

"So what?" She clicked her tongue. "That still counts as millennial."

"So, Dante Huxley is here deadass for reals, you say?" I sighed.

"I heard the news on Andy Silver's radio show!" Angelica clapped her hands.

"I thought Andy Silver was better than peddling gossip on his show."

"Hey now, Ted. Andy sounded excited about it too. He said he likes Dante Huxley's music. Andy's cool like that."

"Andy, Andy." I shook my head. "Andy describes his taste in music as *eclectic*. That just means he'll open his earlobes for anybody."

"So what! Inferno is pretty good."

It was my duty to remind Angelica of her place in the world. "Angelica. You work at Deep Down Music."

"Yeah, so?"

"With great power comes great responsibility." I held one finger in the air to emphasize my point. "You, more than anybody, should know that Dante Huxley, Inferno, all that pop stuff, it's worthless. It's not music. It's not even art."

Angelica started to say something in response.

I raised my hand to stop her. I wasn't done yet. "Inferno and pop garbage like that, it's some sounds thrown together to produce a dopamine hit in the unsuspecting listener. It's just some primitive rhythms that teenagers can shake their rear ends to. Dante Huxley and Inferno are barbarians at the musical gates."

"Are you done yet?" Angelica rolled her eyes. Sometimes she forgot I'm her boss.

"Yes, I'm done."

Angelica took a deep breath. "Andy said his sources inform him that Dante Huxley is staying in an Airbnb rental right here in Honey Bay, for three months, after his scandal." She took a deep breath after blurting it all out.

I shook my head. "Scandal? Maybe the scandal of Dante Huxley's limo parking on my lawn?"

"Dante Huxley's limo driver — you — your lawn — Dante's limo — Dante?" Angelica clapped her hands. Her sentence-making skills weren't worthy of applause.

"Calm down and speak your words, Angelica." She was only a week younger than me. It felt like at least a generation of difference between us. Or a century.

"I'll try." She took a deep breath and stared at me like she was about to freedive a reef. "I'm just wondering about why his limo was parked on your lawn. Is he staying in your part of town?"

"Maybe." I shrugged.

Angelica stared at me. For once she hung on my next word. It was a lot more respect than Angelica usually gave me as my so-called lifelong friend. I didn't approve of Dante's music, but I could still enjoy crumbs of his fame.

"He's staying near your house?" Angelica drummed her pen on the counter.

"Better." I nodded confidently. I didn't condone Angelica's obsession with Dante Huxley, but I could milk her starstruck eagerness like it was a big mooing Holstein. "Much better, Angelica. Or much worse."

"Dante Huxley is staying in your upstairs Airbnb apartment? Oh my God!" Angelica screamed at the ceiling.

"The matter is inconsequential to the world of music." I shrugged coolly. I didn't let on how much I enjoyed my sudden celebrity, at least with Angelica. "And we've got customers to take care of."

"We don't have any customers here, Ted." Angelica sighed. She must've seen my frown: she suddenly corrected herself. "I mean we don't have any customers here yet today. That's what I mean." She quickly looked down at the ground, like she was trying to escape the situation.

"Better." I nodded.

"Yeah, sorry." She leaned against the rack of secondhand LPs.

"Hey, if there's time to lean, there's time to clean!" I ducked into my office and shut the door behind me. Angelica didn't even have a chance to make a smartass rebuttal, nor ask any ridiculous questions about Dante Huxley.

That worthless pop star had already infested Angelica's thoughts. For shame. Even Andy Silver, smart, cynical Andy Silver, was all goo-goo over Dante Huxley. I would have to stand alone as Honey Bay's last bulwark of musical taste.

2

Dante

That upstairs apartment wasn't bad for fifteen hundred a month. For that much back in New York, I could've gotten a smelly basement sublet in the Bronx. This place wasn't exactly hopping, but it smelled a lot better than the Bronx. Warm too. And this "one-room sublet" was as big as a full apartment in New York.

My phone beeped with an incoming message. I refused to look at it. I deleted it while averting my eyes just right so I wouldn't have to read any of it.

It must've been either Kate, my former fiancée, or Roland, my former bandmate. Eloping together, but somehow eager to contact me — maybe, just maybe, to ask about Roland's royalty checks. They'd been leaving messages on my phone all day, as if I didn't know what it was about.

Kate and Roland were already sharing a bed, according to the photos on every celebrity gossip website, so why weren't the lovebirds also sharing a phone?

I deleted all the incoming texts and cleared the voicemail without checking it.

My new bedroom's desk stretched out across the width of the window. It overlooked the most idyllic sitcom-opening-credits sort of street. I half-expected Beaver Cleaver and Mike Brady to come biking down the way.

The houses all in a row, the kids on bikes, the swaying palm trees: it was almost too perfect. All that almost compensated for the gruff asshole of a landlord. Almost. I wouldn't have to deal with him. He was probably at that store of his all day long, and I could go out when he was home. It was a nice enough house without his presence.

After the barrage of texts, my phone actually rang. An actual call.

If Roland had the gumption not just to text me but to call me after shacking up with my fiancée— but it wasn't Roland. It was my manager. He wanted his cut of the pie too, but at least he hadn't seduced my fiancée.

"Hey, superstar." Justice's voice was comfortably familiar and slightly insincere. He was the perennial pseudo-friend who's not a terrible person but is always looking to get something from you. Of course, as my manager, it was his job to be my paid pseudo-friend, so I couldn't complain much.

"What's up, Justice."

"Are you still kicking?" He had that gravelly North Jersey voice of most New York talent managers.

"Yeah. Don't worry. I'm alive and kicking in Honey Bay. You haven't lost your meal ticket."

"Is the apartment alright?" Justice always worried about having done something wrong — something that would cost him his cushy six-figure job.

"It's— it's— it's mostly alright." The place was fine, actually. Just the landlord. "For the most part. Generally."

"Oh shit, is something wrong? Airbnb has an anti-fraud hotline. If the place is not what it's supposed to be, I can contact them—"

"It's good. It's good." I sighed and adjusted the A/C vent on the wall. "Don't worry. I'll survive here."

"I already prepaid the whole three months to Airbnb, but Airbnb only pays the landlord month by month, so really, let me know if something's wrong with the place."

"Nothing's wrong with the place, exactly. Nice and big. Beautiful neighborhood. It's amazing what you can get for fifteen hundred a month here in the Florida boonies."

"But you sounded hesitant?" I could see Justice twirling his pen at his desk, worried about me being unhappy about something.

"The landlord here seems like a bit of a jerk. Or a lot of a jerk. That's all. I don't have to see much of him though, so it doesn't matter."

"I can talk to Airbnb—"

"No, no, just don't worry about it. For now." I sighed. "I'll just avoid him. He says he's out at work all day anyway. I don't think I'll be seeing him often."

"That's good. So you sound like you're doing better? Getting over things?" He was definitely trying to steer the conversation where he'd been trying to steer every conversation of the past week: me reconciling with my former bandmate who'd run off with my former girlfriend.

"Justice. I know where this conversation is going."

"You can't be on non-speaking terms with Roland forever."

"Oh yes I fucking can. Inferno is my band." I tapped my fingers on the desk like I was playing the keyboards. "Roland can go get fucked. By Kate. Who I'm sure is fucking him right at this very moment. I'm not going to be speaking with Roland, playing with him, performing with him, meeting with him, nothing, zero."

"But Inferno, the band — Roland has an ownership share. You can't just kick him out of the band. Inferno is his too."

"I'm not quite sure I remember what Inferno is." I paused for effect, like I was trying to remember who Roland even was. "Maybe it's a band I was in with some guy named Roland. Long ago. In the past. I'm not in that band anymore. So I don't really care what's happening with Inferno. Thanks for asking."

"You're leaving Inferno?"

"Leaving? I already left."

"You can't—"

"Yes I can, Justice. I can do anything I want. I'm the star." I stood up from the desk, just to assert myself to the world. "Roland can see how well Inferno works without Dante."

"You're leaving the band you founded just because of what Roland did?"

"I don't take betrayal lightly, Justice." I breathed deeply. It was easier not to dwell on what Roland and Kate had done. "The lies and deception. Why didn't Kate just break up with me like a decent person? Why was she sneaking around with my bandmate? And Roland — he wouldn't even be famous if it weren't for me — and he was always lying to me about where he was going at night?"

"So you'll leave Inferno to Roland? Isn't that giving him the band?"

"Let him have it." I sat down on my bed, trying to relax. "Maybe he can hire Kate to strut around on stage instead of me."

"And your music career, Dante? That Inferno money's not gonna last you for life. You can't just walk out on your career."

"My money is not gonna last *you* for life, don't you mean, Justice?" I laughed. There was nothing wrong with my manager looking out for his own pocketbook. He always was, anyway.

"I admit I'm concerned about my financial situation. But it's not just me. It's you too, Dante. Inferno is all you have."

"I'll go solo. I'll start a solo career. *Myself* is all I have." I stood up on tiptoe, barefoot, for just a second. I was that much taller. And I was free of that band and all that nonsense now. It was my declaration of independence. "No more Roland. And no more Kate either."

"You're sure? It's a big change. It's a longshot bet." The term "longshot bet" was Justice's way of telling me an idea was crazy. As usual. "Are you really sure you can handle the change?"

Justice had told me the same "longshot bet" schtick three years back when I told him that I was naming the band *Inferno*.

"I don't lie, Justice. When I say something, it's the truth. Unlike Roland and Kate. I don't sneak around lying to people and breaking promises. So yeah. I'm sure I can handle the change."

"Alright." Justice took a deep breath. He seemed more apprehensive than I was. He had the right to be: I controlled my success, and he for the most part had to be along for the ride. "I can start working that solo musician singer-songwriter angle. I can get you some interviews, get you on Colbert, Kimmel—"

"No, no." I tapped my fingers on the desk again. "I need time. I need time so my name isn't synonymous with being the dumbass pop star from Inferno whose fiancée hooked up with his bandmate."

"The media forgets quickly, Dante. They'll be on to the next scandal next week."

"Maybe yes, maybe no. They'll hound me for months if they feel like it. And I also need to come up with some new solo material."

"Got it. Alright. I can see your point of view." That was Justice's way of saying he disagreed but he'd go along with something. "So, how long do you figure—"

"Don't bug me, man." I laughed. Justice meant well. I needed him. But I'd set my own pace. "Give me a little breathing room over here, ok? I'm in Honey Bay for three months, right? That should be enough. Let's see."

"If that annoying landlord doesn't chase you away sooner."

"Yeah. Good point." I stared down the street: no sign of Ted, nor his ridiculous paleolithic orange Range Rover. He probably secretly listened to New Kids On The Block in that thing. "I should have a good few months of restarting my career out here in Honey Bay. If I can put up with the landlord."

"I'll leave you to it, then."

"Thanks for calling. Thanks for caring, Justice." He did care about me, even if it ran parallel to caring about his paycheck. "I'm gonna go on a walk around this little shithole town to clear my head."

"Wear a hoodie and sunglasses," Justice said. "You know, star-in-hiding mode."

"Not sure if I even need that. Like, I'm sure they know who Dante Huxley is out here, but I don't think they'd suspect that Dante Huxley would be walking down the street."

"Do as you please." Justice laughed. "Just be careful not to be stalked by a million fangirls. Or maybe that's what you need after that breakup."

I sighed and clicked off the conversation.

Maybe in a place like Honey Bay, I could go around without being instantly recognized. I could pretend to be an average Honey-Bayian out on a midday walk.

Still in front of the bedroom mirror, I popped up the hood on the hoodie. I tied it a bit. It was probably eighty degrees outside, but I needed my privacy.

My room door locked: check.

Downstairs house door locked: check.

Stupid anti-cat gate closed: check.

That feline testament to gourmet dining lounged on the living room sofa. She didn't look like she was going anywhere from there, with or without a gate.

The breeze outside went right through my hoodie, but in the most pleasant way. It was totally unlike New York's icy winters and its hundred-degree summers.

Even the sun in Honey Bay was more bark than bite: all brilliant shine, without even being burningly hot. The place was perfect —

for a bumfuck small town, anyway, one inhabited by a pretentious know-it-all landlord.

I walked in the same direction Ted had gone to work. That had to be where the main drag was. There wasn't any urban skyline to walk toward, but I could make out a street of shops and pedestrians.

The sign extending from the building said *Deep Down Music*. Same place as on the keychain. Vinyl record sign hanging from a rod on the outside wall like a dangling dick. That had to be Ted's shop.

I pulled my hoodie strings tighter.

Inside the store, Ted stood at the counter the same way he'd been standing at the window when I'd first arrived at his house. Minus the dangling dick.

I kept my hands in my pockets and browsed the aisles. It was amazing that Ted was able to keep a viable business selling this stuff. This was not anything anyone would be buying. It was music that music nerds would talk about over a beer, without even actually having bought it themselves.

Seriously, a used vinyl of *Oar* by Skip Spence? Then a whole bin of Alex Chilton cassettes? This was the kind of shit that made music obsessives horny, but there was no way anybody was buying it. Maybe the guy was so grumpy because he wasn't actually selling any product in his so-called *store*.

Ted was sauntering around his store, guarding his precious inventory and sending suspicious side-eye looks at the few customers present — as if anyone had any interest in stealing a box set of the Buzzcocks that he'd priced at $119.99.

I didn't know whether to laugh or cry at Ted.

Dude was batshit.

3

Ted

A woman ran up to the counter where I stood every day to dispense musical advice. *Ted's Altar*, Angelica called it.

"Hey, I was looking in the *I* section, and then in the *D* section, but I didn't see any Inferno? Dante's Inferno?"

"Did you say *Inferno*?" I couldn't help but smirk. I liked to rub it in customers' faces a little bit that we didn't sell the kind of crap they might have been accustomed to buying at other so-called music stores. "Are you sure you have that artist name right?"

"Yeah. Inferno." She looked back over her shoulder, at the shelves of quality music I'd painstakingly curated. She had zero appreciation or even cognition of their worth. Her mind was already in the musical dump. "There wasn't anything under *Dante's Inferno* either."

"Why would I be selling that stuff?" I took a deep breath and shook my head. "This is a *music* store. I don't sell Inferno."

"Come on, Inferno! They're awesome. Remember their song, 'That's How I Shake It'?" She held her hands up in the air like she was dancing.

"That's all it's good for." I sighed. "Standing around on an otherwise perfectly acceptable Tuesday morning. Waving your hands around. And dancing."

"I heard that Dante Huxley is actually visiting—" she was spouting off, rapid-fire. Her eyes opened in obvious excitement.

I stopped her before she could start telling me about my own tenant. "If you want that kind of crap, Dante Huxley or Dante's Inferno or whatever, go home and download it off streaming."

I turned my back to her. I preferred to face the wall.

"I was just trying to support a local business." She sounded more indignant than apologetic.

"I'll have you know." I turned to face her. "I, unlike the streaming services where you get your music, unlike all the quote unquote musical artists you listen to — I care about music. Music *qua* music. Do you understand?"

She was still staring at me. Maybe the message was getting across.

I continued. "And no matter how much filthy lucre anyone offers me, I won't be selling Inferno or any of that bubble-gum garbage. If you're looking for Inferno, I suggest you just march out of here, because this isn't your kind of store. Thank you and goodbye."

I turned back to face the wall again. At least the wall didn't ask me to stock Inferno albums.

The woman stomped out, all boots clacking on my hardwood floors. Good riddance.

"You don't like Inferno? Seems pretty harsh." The gray hoodie at the back of the store popped off the head it was resting on. It was that tenant: Dante Huxley. He must've come after asking around town for the best music store in Honey Bay. Or in all east-central Florida, in fact.

"Believe it or not, we music aficionados are entitled to our opinions." I gritted my teeth. "That must surprise you, since the only opinions you must encounter are those of your clueless adoring fans that you lead like sheep to the pseudo-musical slaughter?"

"Ah, no. Relax, man. I'm open-minded about music." Dante shook his head and laughed, his perfectly white teeth on display. As if what we were discussing were a laughing matter. "I like all kinds of music. I'm all for musical debate, compare and contrast, what have you."

"Really? Compare and contrast?" I sighed. "How can that be possible when you haven't even heard real music? What are you going to be comparing and contrasting? 98 Degrees and Boyzone? You must have no inkling of the kinds of music we have here at Deep Down." I gestured to him: the expanse of musical recordings I held in my store's inventory.

"You sell some great stuff." He nodded. It was probably some weird sort of Gen Z sarcasm. "It's impossible these days to find a physical music store that would actually stock an Alex Chilton album."

"Alex Chilton?" I stepped back from Dante. I was shocked enough by that name-drop to be almost scared of this Dante guy. How could anyone with poofy hair know this? "You've heard of Alex Chilton?"

"Of course I know Alex Chilton." Now Dante was the one looking at me like I was crazy. "What pop musician doesn't know Alex Chilton?" A half-smile cracked across Dante's mouth. Half-dimples formed in his cheeks.

I found myself staring at Dante. My thigh found my dick half-erect. My mouth threw itself into autopilot. "See, if you want to do anything in pop music, you have to know Alex Chilton. He pretty much invented modern pop rock. Go listen to some Alex Chilton." I was starting in on the lecture I'd prepared to give in response to Dante saying he'd never heard of Alex Chilton.

Except that wasn't what Dante had said. That wasn't the lecture I should've been giving. Dante was way ahead of me. He probably knew more about Alex Chilton than I did.

"Yeah, Alex Chilton and Big Star. I never go far without a little Big Star." Dante laughed and gave a thumbs-up. "I already have all of Alex Chilton's albums on my laptop. If I didn't, I'd buy one to support your store."

"Well you *should* be supporting our store." I remembered my proper role: I was supposed to be burying Dante Huxley, not praising him. "The garbage melodies you sell couldn't even exist without standing on the shoulders of real music. You pop stars are parasites on the musical world."

"I think you're pretty delusional about that part." Dante shook his head and snickered right in my face. "The music I make isn't garbage just because people buy it. Just because it's not, you know, a Sigur Ros album that like twenty people buy."

"You know Sigur Ros?" I shook my head. There was no way this bouffanted pretty boy had any idea of—

"Yeah, man. Check out my playlist." Dante held his phone up to my face. "Listening to the Sigur Ros founder's solo album now. Jonsi. He went solo. I've been doing some research on lead singers going solo."

"How could you produce your kind of bubble-gum trash if you're aware of music like Sigur Ros and Jonsi?" I shook my head at him in pity. "You've seen the stars in the sky and still you insist on swimming in the gutter."

"I think there's a faulty assumption here, my man." Dante popped his hoodie back up over his overstyled hair. "Inferno isn't bubble-gum trash. A piece of music isn't bubble-gum trash just because people, you know, actually go out and buy it. Have you ever listened to our music? Any Inferno albums? At all?"

"Not voluntarily, no. Maybe unwillingly caught a few seconds walking by a dance club in Fort Lauderdale." I winced as I shook my head. "But voluntarily, I would not be caught dead listening to crud like Inferno."

"Then there's your problem." Dante laughed again.

He was laughing in my face. In a discussion about music. In a musical discussion, this musical nobody, this ingenue, this *foundling*, was asserting his imagined authority over me.

"I think you need to listen to some Inferno albums without your negative preconceptions," Dante continued. "Then judge it however you might."

Dante's brilliant blue-green eyes flitted around my store. He was probably taking inventory. Maybe he was collecting names of bands he could name-drop in his next conversation with a real music expert. To my surprise, I didn't mind, not as long as I could keep checking out those beautiful eyes of his.

"Is that all, Dante?" I asked, disdain laced into my voice. As beautiful as his appearance was, his musical sensibility was beyond explanation or redemption.

"Actually, the name of your store." Dante pointed up at the sign hanging from the outside wall. "Deep Down Music."

"Yeah, you probably have no idea." I sighed. Some knowledge was just way out of reach for someone like him. "You have no idea what it refers to."

"Is it a reference to Muddy Waters? His song 'Deep Down In Florida?'" Dante made an anguished guitar-playing face and picked at an imaginary blues guitar. For a twenty something-year-old blond pop star, he did a frighteningly good impression of Muddy Waters.

"How could you possibly know 'Deep Down In Florida?' That song?" I didn't know whether to be impressed or intrigued. The kid wasn't as dumb as he looked. Or he was some kind of spy. "Did Angelica tell you?"

"What?"

"My assistant." I pointed over at Angelica, dusting shelves of vinyls in the corner. She gave a small wave. "Did she tell you that I named the store after that Muddy Waters song?"

"Uh, no. I never talked to her." Dante shook his head. His neck was perfectly shaped, like the neck of a statue, a beautiful man in profile. And for some reason, my dick was also as hard as a marble statue. "Come on, I'm in the music industry. Even if I'm in bubblegum pop. Of course I know Muddy Waters."

"And you know the song 'Deep Down In Florida'?"

"We're deep down in Florida, aren't we?" Dante laughed again. The way he threw his head back — he looked like he was in the middle of an orgasm. "It was one of the first songs Muddy Waters made with Johnny Winter. The album was called — what was it called — *Hard Again*."

I gulped. My knees weakened. "Yeah. *Hard Again*."

"Great album." Dante held two thumbs up. "And hey, go listen to some Inferno. It's a lot better than you expect."

"Yeah, whatever." I turned my back to him and went back to my air-conditioned office. He muttered something. I let him have the last word.

The seven hours before I went home were plenty of time for Dante to pack up and leave. Good riddance. Maybe this just wasn't working out.

I closed up shop half an hour early, as soon as dark set down on Honey Bay. It had been a slow day, and evenings were always slowest.

Back home, the gate was open. The same gate I'd told Dante to keep closed.

I rushed into the house.

Dante was milling around the kitchen. The house smelled like charcoal, grilled meat, and barbeque sauce.

"The gate. You didn't close the gate. Where's the cat?"

"Oh." Dante's face filled with shock. He shook his head. "I'm sorry. Very sorry about that." His apology actually sounded sincere. "I forgot to close the gate. But don't worry. Duchess has been hanging out with me here on the patio all afternoon."

"Oh. Ok." I breathed a bit of relief. "I need to give her dinner."

"I won't stop you from feeding her, but I might have given her a bite of grilled chicken. Or three. Or maybe a whole drumstick."

"You've been grilling?"

"Sorry, did I overstep the rules?" His face was full of apology. "I thought I was allowed to use the grill."

"Oh yeah, you are. I was just asking." I calmed myself down. I didn't need to be on full alert around him all the time. "I'm just getting used to having someone around here."

"In fact." Dante pulled a towel off a plastic-wrapped plate. "I made you dinner: barbecue chicken thighs." He presented the plate to me with two hands, like a formal offering.

Dante was not a bad guy. And I'd been a jerk to him. For good reason. But still, a jerk.

"Oh. Thanks but no. I— I, uh, I already had dinner at the store." That made no sense. But I would've been uncomfortable accepting dinner from the guy I'd just chewed out, the same guy whose rent money was saving my house from foreclosure. "I think I'm going to — go take a nap. A nap."

"Alright. Nothing wrong with napping. It's one of my favorite activities too." Dante nodded. "You don't mind if I feed Duchess the chicken thighs I grilled for you?"

"I would appreciate that as much as she would. Would save me the trouble of having to open a can of food for her dinner." Duchess was already staring at the unwrapped plate of chicken thighs I'd set down on the patio table. "Thank you, from me and her." I went back inside, then upstairs.

After a shower and a nap in my room, I came back downstairs. Duchess was sleeping on the living room sofa, her usual hangout.

Dante wasn't there. He'd probably left a huge mess for me to clean up on the patio. I knew what spoiled prettyboys like that were like.

Except he hadn't left any mess. The patio was perfectly clean. He'd even put the barbeque sauce back in the refrigerator.

Maybe these three months weren't going to be so bad.

I grabbed a chilled bottle of Duvel from the refrigerator and my tablet from its charger. After a whole day of retail endeavors, I could indulge my senses of smell and taste with fine Belgian ale, and my libido with some choice websites.

The video I chose was pretty good. Just softcore. Close-ups of guys slowly soaping up their asses under beach showers, stuff like that.

Warm tablet resting against my cock and dude-ass all over the screen, I got hard. That was a bit of a problem. With a tenant in residence, I couldn't just jack off. It was my patio, but still. That part of my evening routine would have to change with a tenant in house. Had I remembered the no-fap zone that my patio had become, I would've devoted less of my upstairs time to napping.

"Hey, what's up." Dante was approaching from the living room. Good thing I wasn't stroking my dick like a zoo chimp.

"Hello, Dante." I toasted him with my glass of beer. "Can I pour you a glass of fine Belgian ale?"

"Wow." He smiled and nodded. "You are a connoisseur indeed. Belgian ale sounds excellent."

I grabbed a second glass from the cabinet and poured for him. The head — the creamy white foam— reminded me of— I had to calm my breathing, shut down my degenerate thoughts, and just give Dante his beer.

"Good beer. Damn. Really good beer." He took a big chug. "I know music, but I guess I don't know beer. I didn't even know beer like this existed. You're a true connoisseur."

"You said it yourself." It felt good to be appreciated. "I'm a connoisseur."

"Dude." Dante looked over at my tablet and laughed. "I don't mean to be nosy. But like, are you also a connoisseur of naked guys?"

"Why do you ask?" I raised my eyebrows just a little.

"Just saying." Dante took another sip of his beer and laughed. He glanced over at my tablet again. "You're looking at naked dudes on your tablet. That just seems kind of gay."

I hadn't even thought to hide what was on my screen. But there was no way to hide my gayness, nor any reason. Let the fallout fall where it may.

"I'm gay." I looked at Dante for a reaction. "And not just kind of gay. I'm full-on homogay."

"Like — for real?" He didn't seem shocked. His eyebrows were raised again. "Full-on gay?"

"For real." I held the tablet screen in his direction. He could verify for himself the ten and a half inches of manflesh it retina-displayed. "I look at some naked dude-flesh to relax. Probably the same way you look at women's titties."

"Oh." He looked me up and down. "So. That, like, means you're attracted to dudes? Sexually? Like, you're interested in sex with men?"

"I do believe that's how being full-on homogay works, yeah." I took another sip of my beer. I felt the least apologetic, embarrassed, or secretive I'd ever felt about revealing my orientation. Maybe it was because I'd hit thirty. I just didn't owe the world anything. I was gay and that was it.

Dante was looking at me and nodding to himself. "Huh."

"If you have a problem living here because I'm gay, that's fine. I'll understand. I'll refund your money."

"No, no. Not at all. Not like that." His hand flew up. "I don't have anything against it. It's just not something I was expecting. A gay landlord. I didn't think you're gay."

"Alright." I shrugged. "Well now you know. I'm gay."

"So do you like—" The embarrassed look on his eyes suggested he was going to ask whether I liked to take it up the ass. That was always the first question. As if that was what being gay was all about. Or maybe that was in fact what being gay was all about. "Do you like—"

"Do I like dicks up my ass?" I laughed. "That's what straight men always ask me about being gay."

"No!" Dante spat beer on the patio floor. He grabbed a paper towel and mopped it up. "I was just going to ask you if you have like a husband or boyfriend."

"Oh. Sorry. My mind was running a bit." It was. Even if Dante was straight, talking about dicks and ass with him was kind of a turn-on. "Nope. No boyfriend, no husband. Never had either. Just single and all alone here in this small town." I was getting comfortable in this conversation. I leaned my head back and laughed. "Honey Bay is not the most active social scene. For anybody. As you might have figured out already."

"So you're just a single gay dude, living in Honey Bay, running a music store?" Dante's face suggested he was looking at a museum display of exotic penguins. "And you're, like, sexually attracted to men."

"I believe so." I sighed and gulped down the last of my beer. "I believe that's how it works."

4

Dante

How would it feel to wake up in a man's arms?

Did men kiss when they woke up together?

What if they both had morning hard-ons?

Kate had always slapped away my morning hard-ons, like they were a crime. Would it have been different with a dude?

Every morning, Ted cooed "good morning" to Duchess. It was loud enough for me to hear through the walls. He spent the first few minutes of his day sweet-talking to her.

And every morning, I wondered how I'd feel if that "good morning" had been directed to me. What if he sweet-talked like that at me?

Did gay guys say sweet things to each other? Did they kiss?

From my bed I could hear him showering. Did gay dudes stroke their dicks in the shower just to admire their erections in the mirror?

In my fantasies Ted did that. He always did that. He played with his cock in the shower until it was hard, then pumped and squeezed it until it shot all over the shower wall. Then he cleaned the sticky stuff off the shower tile by rubbing his wet ass against it.

I pretended to be still asleep when Ted left for work every day at ten. As soon as the front door closed, I rose up in bed just enough to be able to see him out the window, getting into his orange Range Rover.

He always wore shorts. His calves always flexed as he climbed up into the seat. I'd never noticed how a man's calves were so perfectly sculpted. I'd never seen a woman with calves like that. The fuzzy brown hair extending down from his shorts all the way to his socks was even more exciting.

I couldn't believe I was staring.

After staring, I had to jack off. Just had to. Sometimes twice. Not thinking about anything. Not letting myself think about anything: only the physical sensation. Then I contemplated how I'd spend my day so I wouldn't have to face Ted when he came home around seven.

Honey Bay Fitness, just down the street, was happy to have me. They were open until midnight. Perfect timing for my avoiding Ted in the evenings.

If only not thinking of Ted had been as easy as not catching sight of him. In the gym showers, I caught myself staring at dicks and asses and mentally comparing them to Ted. Or what little I'd seen of Ted naked in his window that morning, plus what my imagination made up and filled in.

Why was I doing this?

That first morning, I hadn't yet trained my eyes to take in male beauty. He was just some naked dude with a dangling dick. Now, a week later, that dangling dick of Ted's was all I thought about when I let my thoughts run idle — though in my fantasies, it wasn't ever just idly dangling.

The dude in front of me in the cardio room had a big meaty ass. In his tight pink shorts, it looked like a rising sun.

A lot of men had big meaty asses. They looked like fucking filet mignons. Why hadn't I ever noticed before? Why had I not even paid attention?

Ted's ass was a lot more compact. When he walked in jeans, the sinewy muscle was obvious.

Why the fuck was I thinking about this?

My phone rang.

"Justice. What's up." I slowed down on the elliptical.

"You're breathing hard. Getting it on with a new woman bright and early at eight A.M.?" Justice burst into laughter.

"Appreciate the good humor. I'm on the elliptical trainer. What's up?"

"Are we on speakerphone?" Justice asked warily. My theory was that he was projecting himself into the spy thrillers he loved to read. He always thought our bullshit talks were top secret.

"No, we're not. I'm wearing headphones. Nobody can hear you." I indulged his spy fetish. "I'm in the middle of the cardio room, but things seem pretty secure here."

"So you're getting settled in Honey Bay?"

"It's been a week, yeah." I sped up my elliptical pumping a little. If we were just having small talk, I didn't need to be slowing down.

"Been writing new songs for your solo breakout?"

"No, no, man." I audibly sighed as best I could through my cardio-quickened breaths. "It's only been a week. Let me decompress a little."

"Yeah, understood." He sounded disappointed. "Is that landlord pretty ok then?"

"What do you mean, *pretty ok*?" My stomach tensed. Then my jaw. Had Justice somehow read my thoughts?

"You know, not annoying you too much?"

"Oh." I eased up. He meant like that. "Yeah. He's fine." I gulped, wishing I could take that back. "I mean, it's fine."

"How are you spending your days? Just hanging out?"

"What are you, the daily agenda police?" I laughed at my own joke, even if Justice didn't. "I'm spending them like I'm spending them."

"I mean, I hope you're feeling better. Catching a second wind."

"Definitely. Justice, are you in a hot tub right now?"

"Yeah, why?"

"I hear the bubbles. It's a little unprofessional, isn't it?" I loved putting him on the spot, in the pettiest ways.

"I'm going to — um, have a meeting here. Business."

"Alright, man." I laughed. "I believe you. A hundred percent."

"Good to hear you're doing ok, Dante. Take care of yourself. Do you need anything from me?"

"I was just thinking — if I go solo — Justice, have you ever questioned — I mean, did it ever make you wonder — ah, never mind."

"What?"

"Don't worry. My thoughts wander while I exercise. Talk to you later."

"Alright!"

Justice clicked off the phone. He usually called at the end of the month if I hadn't been in touch, likely just to make sure I hadn't died, and that his monthly salary transfer was still on the way.

I got into the Uber at nine fifty A.M. When I arrived back home, Ted's Range Rover was still in the driveway. He hadn't left for the day. I was risking an awkward encounter.

I rushed into the house, as quietly as I could, and stealth-walked upstairs to my room. I didn't have to face Ted. I didn't have to think about Ted. At least not any more than I already did.

Not until five minutes later.

He banged his fist on my door.

I opened.

He was dressed for work, though his hair was wet and he was barefoot.

"I'm trying to go to work, Dante. I have a day job, you know. I'm trying to go to work."

"And? Did I wake you up when I was going out to the gym?"

"No." Ted pointed down the stairs. "I'm leaving for work, and look, the gate is open! I don't know if you were coming or going, but the gate is open."

"I'm sorry, Ted. I'm sorry. I must've forgotten."

"Sorry?" He raised his hands in the air, the same way he'd done when he had a fit at my limo driver on my first day. "What good is *sorry* when I'm trying to go to work, and instead of going to work, I have to spend fifteen minutes looking for Duchess, inside and outside?"

"Duchess always stays in your room in the mornings, Ted. Come on." I sighed and pointed in her direction. "We're not living in a nuclear bunker here. Fine, I left the gate open once. I'm sorry. Fine."

"Once? It definitely is not the first time." Ted tapped his hairy hand on my room's door. It was his door. I guess he had the right. He smelled like fresh soap and shampoo, and his beefy arm banging my door like that was the sexiest thing I'd seen in a long time.

"I apologized, Ted." I stepped half a step closer to him. "I apologized to you already. I can't go back in time and fix my mistake. Look, it's a gate door, the cat didn't run out, everything is good."

"Everything is good when I'm fifteen minutes, now half an hour late to work? And I'm perspiring before even leaving the house, because I'm worried about Duchess, because you can't even be bothered to close the gate? So everything is good, you say?"

Ted stared at me, looking for an answer. His brown eyes were huge in all his flurry of anger. He folded his arms across his chest: maybe he carried album shelves all day, because his arms were solid muscle. I hadn't noticed that.

"Maybe, Mister Dante Huxley, when you're a boy band star with no job and no responsibilities, everything seems good."

"You really—" I stared at him, shaking my head. I tried to be angry at him. I drew up all the anger I could muster. He was a pretentious jerk, after all. He'd insulted my music and my career. He'd treated me, a paying customer of his rental, as an unwelcome intruder. But all that came to mind was how beautiful he looked with his half-dried hair and polo shirt and board shorts, how even his morning hissy fit was sexy.

"I really what?" He unfolded his arms and put his hands on his hips.

"You really should—" I took one step toward him.

"I really should what?"

"You really should—" I took a bigger step toward him, until we stood chest to chest. My heart raced. I'd never been close like that with a dude, not any dude. Especially not a dude who I wanted to— "You really should kiss me," I blurted. I moved my mouth closer to him.

Ted wrapped his arms around me. He brought his lips to mine. His breath smelled like toothpaste.

Up close, Ted's face wasn't as smooth as I'd expected: it was full of tiny scruff and whiskers. He looked even manlier. My dick sprung to erection.

His lips were soft. Delicious. What kind of idiot had I been all my life, thinking a man's lips couldn't have been pleasant to kiss?

I went with it. I opened my mouth. He rubbed his scrubby upper lip against my face, then his cheek. He kissed me and his tongue went inside me. His hands were all over my back.

Mechanically speaking, it wasn't very different from kissing a woman. Lips were lips, tongue was tongue — but this was actually exciting. My heart raced unlike anything I'd ever felt with a woman.

He half-closed his eyes. I put my tongue deep into his mouth. This was really happening. I was kissing a man. He squeezed both of my hands in his hands, then held on to them.

My breathing was fast. So was his. I could barely stand. My dick wanted to jump out of my pants. I tried not to be shy about rubbing my crotch up against Ted. So what if it was gay? That was the point.

He opened his eyes and stared at me. His face was full of fear. Maybe he was even more scared than I was.

He stepped back and let go of my hands. He gulped and blinked. It must've felt like a dream for him too.

He shook his head. "I have to go. I have to go to work now."

He was headed downstairs before I even caught my breath. I could only yell after him: "Remember to close the gate."

I made myself laugh. My head was woozy. Maybe it was the morning workout, or maybe it was everything that had just happened. My life felt like someone else's life, or a completely new existence. I'd broken up with Kate. I'd quit Inferno. I'd just kissed a man.

I needed to lie down. I closed my eyes. My hard dick tented my jeans, and the thin comforter atop them. That hard dick — it was from kissing a man. It was more difficult to believe than anything else, but I was sure about it. I wanted it more than I'd ever wanted anything.

The phone rang again. Kate. Actually calling, not just texting or contacting me through Justice. If nothing else, I admired her chutzpah.

Her name on my phone screen didn't even hurt. She was just a part of my past. Maybe a past mistake.

"Hey Kate. Good morning." It felt like taking a call from a distant relative I talked to once a year out of obligation.

"Dante. I'm sorry about what the press put you through." No mention of her own wrongdoing. No mention of lying to me. No mention of claiming to be "going to bed early" when she was going to Roland's bed. She didn't take any responsibility for it. But I had to remember: she was part of my past. Like all of Inferno.

"Comes with being a celebrity." I kept my answer short. If she was waiting for me to beg to get back together — that wasn't going to happen. "Anything else, Kate?"

"I just thought it would be fair to tell you before the press tells you."

"Yeah?"

"Tomorrow I'm marrying Roland." She sounded like she was confessing to a crime. "We're going to do one of those fake-secret ceremonies where it's leaked to the press. Will get our pictures in all the tabloids. Should help his career and mine."

"Alright." I tapped the air conditioning control from 74 down to 68. I needed to chill in every sense.

"I mean, the press might be hounding you or something, looking for your reaction."

I laughed. "I'm a celebrity, Kate. I know how it goes. You'll find out too."

"Did I— hold on—" She was walking somewhere as she talked. Suddenly the ambient noise died down. She must've stepped into a quiet place. "Did I hurt you? I'm sorry, Dante."

"Did you hurt me?" Did she need to ask? "Nobody likes being lied to, Kate. Nobody likes being treated like a third wheel to the affair you were having. Nobody likes being the last to find out. Other than that, whatever."

"I'm sorry we broke up." What a bizarre thing to say.

"I'm actually fine with that part." I laughed, a little wryly. "Totally fine with that part. You like Roland, you go be with Roland. I just wish you and Roland had any bit of decency about the way you did it."

"We were— I don't know — I wasn't thinking right — it was love."

"Ok. It happened. Anything else?"

"Roland wonders if there's any way you can come back to Inferno."

"Now I know why you called. Now I understand."

"Well, Roland is just wondering—"

"Nope. It's all his. Never performing with him again. Never speaking with him again. Tired of shaking my ass on stage to give Roland a seven-figure paycheck. He can go do his own thing now."

"And Roland's share of the royalties not yet paid out, from before the time you quit—"

"Jesus. Now I know what this call is all about." I rolled my head on my neck. A tension headache was coming on. "Roland will get paid. I'm not a thief. He can contact Justice for the logistics."

"Oh, thanks." Her voice brightened.

"Anything else, Kate?"

"Nope!"

"Alright. Enjoy your wedding tomorrow." I clicked off the phone before she could respond.

I'd be ok. I just needed to rest. From everything.

I started to put my phone away. It rang again. Maybe Kate wanted me to run the royalty calculations for Roland, or double-check that he was getting his portion of the merchandise sales, or ask if I might possibly perform with him in the future—

It wasn't her. It was Justice.

"Solo musicians' league. Dante speaking. How can I help you?"

"Very good. Well played. I wanted to update you on Kate. If you're up for hearing it."

"She already called me."

"She told you about the wedding?"

"She told me about the wedding. Tomorrow."

"Oh. Are you ok?"

"Would've been more ok if her entire call had not been an excuse for her to double-check that we're still going to pay Roland his cut of the royalties. I mean that was the real reason she called."

"She's shameless." Justice laughed. "I thought she'd only ask me that, not you too."

"Oh yeah. I was ready for her to give me Roland's incoming wire transfer information or some shit. Like she thinks I'm going to cheat him."

"Ironic, right?" Justice was kind of smart sometimes.

"After he and she lied and cheated me, yeah, ironic."

"I'm sorry, man. Just look at the bright side though. You're Dante Huxley. You can have pretty much any woman you want."

"Yeah. Whoopty doo." I sighed. "That's, like, the last thing on my mind. Or it's not even on my mind actually."

"What, you turning gay now?" Justice roared in laughter. I didn't answer. "You hear me, Dante? I'm teasing you. Women not on your mind. Are you gay or something?"

"Yeah, you know, Justice. Sometimes stuff happens, and you realize stuff."

"Why are you so serious all of a sudden?" Justice sounded a little hurt. Usually he was the one who dragged me back to serious-land from my joking.

"I just need time by myself."

"So it's not a good time to talk about how we launch your solo career?"

"Yeah, here's how we launch it: give me some quiet time by myself. Alright? Got it?" I was sounding a little like Ted. His annoyed attitude was rubbing off on me. Or maybe Justice was just unquestionably annoying.

"I got you, Dante. I got you. Take your rest time. Just don't turn gay or anything." He laughed again and hung up the phone.

He meant well, even if he didn't really understand me, not one little bit.

I put the phone on mute. I didn't want to talk to anybody. Not Kate, not Justice, not the Grammy committee. Not even Ted.

It was high noon, and I was due for a nap.

When I woke up, the brilliant sun was gone from the sky. The moon was barely visible. It must've been around eight P.M. Somebody — obviously Ted — stood outside my door, maybe trying to listen to what I was up to.

I only went back to sleep. I didn't need any more human interaction.

I woke up again, to thunder on the door. Outside, the midday sun blazed high in the sky. I'd spent twenty-four hours sleeping, just hiding from the world.

"Dante." Ted was at the door. "I'm worried about you, Dante."

I forced myself to swing my legs up and out of bed. Had I stayed in bed any longer, I might've developed pressure ulcers.

I got up and trudged to the door. Ted stood outside, holding a plastic takeout bag. Whatever it was smelled delicious. I was hungry enough that anything edible would've smelled delicious.

"I've got an urgent culinary delivery for the reclusive pop star!" Ted held up the bag. "May I?" He gestured grandiosely at my room, the same way he'd gestured at his precious lawn.

"Yeah. Sure." I rubbed my eyes. This was the man I'd kissed the previous day. I tried not to think about that. I was hungry.

"Sir, may I set the table?" Ted made the same grandiose gesture, this time toward my desk. All that was on it was my laptop, still in its case, and Bluetooth headphones.

"Yes, again." I laughed and nodded. Even if I was trying to avoid Ted, somehow the interaction was helping my mood.

He took one small styrofoam box out of his bag. Then another. Then another. And another.

"I thought you own a music store. But now I think you own a circus."

"What?" Ted started arranging the tiny boxes in rows.

"That takeout bag of yours is like a clown car."

"Oh that." Ted gestured at the rows of tiny styrofoam food boxes on my desk. "Tapas. Enjoy." He reached into the bag again and pulled out actual metal utensils, wrapped in a paper towel.

"Honey Bay has tapas?" I laughed.

"Well, I'm glad at least something made you laugh!" Ted nodded with a smile. "Try some. Olives, mushrooms, garlic shrimp, got anything you want."

"This is all for me?" I had to restrain myself from stuffing the food in my mouth. The smell was irresistible. And I was very hungry.

"Unless the rest of Inferno is hiding under the bed." Ted held up the comforter and peeked under. "Nope. Doesn't look like it. So yeah, all for you."

"Fuck." I laughed and shook my head. "Excuse my language. But care to join me for a tapas dinner?" I grabbed a second chair from up against the wall and pulled it to the desk.

"It's not a requirement or anything. I just wanted to bring you some food. I can leave you to yourself again if that would make you more comfortable." Ted pointed at the door.

"Stay." I suddenly became self-conscious. Ted was a dude. A hot dude. A dude I'd kissed. I couldn't just be smelly around him. "If you don't mind that I smell like a guy who's just spent a day, a night, and a morning sleeping."

"That's quite an accurate way of describing the aroma." Ted's face was about to break into laughter. "But I don't mind. I'm just worried about how you're holding up."

"Not too bad. Nice that you care. Thank you."

"I don't follow celebrity news. But I Googled you just to find out what's going on. Must've been really rough, that break up with your girlfriend. I mean fiancée. I'm sorry."

"You know what I realized?" Self-consciously, I held my arms down, so my armpits wouldn't smell up the room.

"That you were more into the idea of having a relationship than into the relationship itself?" Ted was fucking clairvoyant. Maybe my unshowered smell gave him visions.

"Shit. Yeah. It's kind of like that." I shook my head.

"You know, the way I look at it — if she treated you like that, then be glad you found out now what kind of person she is. Be grateful she let you know early, you know." Ted looked out the window and thought about something. "I'm speaking from experience here. I'm ten years older than you. Thirty-two now."

"The way we—" I didn't know how to say it without actually saying it, so I just said it. "The way we kissed yesterday. I never kissed like that with Kate. I never felt that kind of passion."

"Yeah." Ted nodded. "It doesn't really sound like you were that close with Kate."

"I wasn't." My relationship with her always seemed like something we were doing more for the cameras than for ourselves. We were always trying to be seen together somewhere, so we'd stay in the celebrity news cycle.

"I figured you were hibernating up in your room because of me," Ted said.

"Because of you?" I looked at him, eyebrows up.

"I mean, we had our kiss, you didn't know what it means, you're thinking about me, that kind of thing." Ted must have thought that men fell over themselves for him every day.

"Not really." I laughed. I looked directly at him to let him know I meant it. "It wasn't really that. It was still the pain of betrayal."

"Oh. Yeah." Ted looked down at his hands folded in his lap. "Not everything is about me. I have to remember that."

"It wasn't about anybody, really. It was just about the pain of betrayal. That I thought I knew what was going on in my band and in my life, but really, I had no idea. All those times I thought Roland was at the gym and Kate was sleeping at her apartment — it's like I was living in a fictional reality."

"Yeah." Cautiously, gingerly, Ted wrapped his arm around me. It felt like all the love and support I could possibly want. "Sometimes discovering something like that is like growing up again, when you're already an adult."

"Kate and Roland, both of them were nobodies when they first met me." I exhaled deeply. "That doesn't mean I own them. I don't expect gratitude. I don't need to be thanked. I just expect to be treated a little bit honestly and decently, you know?"

"I know what you mean. Don't need to be a celebrity to know betrayal." He squeezed me tighter and ran his hand up and down my arm. Whatever that was, it was what I'd been waiting for all that time.

"Kate called me." I pointed at my phone. "She called me like just to chat, but then you know what?"

"Let me guess." Ted cleared his throat. "Money?"

"Bingo!" I laughed up at the ceiling. "She was calling to make sure that Roland would still be getting paid by the band."

"Shit."

"Of course Roland will be getting paid. Business is business. I'm not a thief. Just funny that Roland getting paid was the first thing, the only thing, on Kate's mind." I bit my lower lip and shook my head.

"Well now you're free of all that." Ted grabbed my arm in his hand and shook it up and down, like he was trying to kick-start my recovery. "And you've got tapas."

"Will the tapas survive if I take a quick shower?" I looked over the selection of boxes and cups Ted had brought. My desk looked like a chessboard. "I smell like a Spanish bullfighter."

"Well, the gate downstairs is closed." Ted smiled at me. "I don't think the tapas will run away."

"I'll be fast." I speed-walked the three long steps to my bathroom. Inside, I speed-showered, smelling myself every few seconds. After a round of shampoo and body wash, I was satisfied with my smell, or lack thereof.

I didn't look half-bad in the mirror. I'd always been afraid of checking out my body in the mirror. It was kind of gay. But now, well — whatever Kate had said about me getting a beer belly was bullshit. I didn't look half-bad in the mirror.

I hadn't brought a change of clothes into the bathroom. I'd have to just walk out wearing a towel. I opened the door to my room and walked out. I wasn't wearing a towel.

"Hot damn." Ted's face turned red. "Now you're naked."

"Not naked. Nude." I stepped closer to him. Water was dripping off of me. I hadn't even bothered to towel dry. "The word is *nude*."

"You're my tenant." Ted shook his head. "I really don't want to—" His gaze focused directly on my cock. His fascination with it was fucking hot. My dick rose up as he stared at it.

I stood next to him and jerked my dick a little to make it harder. "You're a cock connoisseur?" I sat down right next to him.

He gulped and stared at me naked. "Hot damn, part two."

His words and the stare of his big brown eyes made my cock and balls tingle. I'd never been so horny for any woman. "I can't believe how much I'm getting turned on by getting checked out by a dude."

"Good lord." Ted shook his head while looking at me. "It's not just that you're a celebrity. But your face is gorgeous. And that lily-white body, the muscles, and your ass. Like too good to be true."

"Ted. I can tell you a secret."

5

Ted

When Dante walked out of the shower naked, ninety-nine percent of my blood had already gone to my nether regions.

I managed enough control over my muscles and face to smile at him. "Is your secret that you're a figment of my lonely gay fantasies?"

"Nope. I'm real." He stood up right in front of me, then wrapped his skinny long fingers around his skinny long dick. Miraculously, he was uncut. Precum glistened around the purple-pink dickhead and crown of foreskin. My mouth salivated. I almost drooled.

"You're real." I had to say something. Maybe to stop myself from fainting.

"My dick is real too." Holding the middle of the shaft and moving it up and down, Dante jacked it slowly. He stared into my eyes while he played with himself.

"You're my tenant. You just had a breakup." I shook my head. I was talking to myself more than to him. "I shouldn't."

"Or maybe you should." Dante grinned down at his hard dick and shook his head side-to-side.

I swallowed air. I ran my eyes up and down him. I didn't have to be ashamed. He was obviously showing off.

"What's your secret anyway?" I asked him. All I needed to know about him was already hard and pointed at my face.

"My secret is — I've been checking you out every morning when you go to work. I've been staring at you. Admiring your ass. And jerking off, every fucking time." Dante pumped his dick harder with his hand. Precum dripped out onto his shaft. He smiled as he looked down at his dick in his hand.

"Holy fuck." He'd been checking me out. As much as I liked to pretend otherwise, I was just a music store owner in a small town. I stared at his dick. It was like he was standing to flaunt his hardness directly in my face. "Dante? Can I?" I asked without taking my eyes off his cock.

"You can, but may you?" Dante wagged it back and forth in front of my face. A drop of precum flew off and landed on my shirt.

"May I?" I breathed quickly while staring at Dante's cockhead. I could almost taste his dick. I'd never felt desire like that.

"Indeed." Dante stepped toward me, cradling his cock in his hands. He was presenting it to my mouth like a trophy. "You may."

I lay my hand under his hand and took the dickhead up to my lips. I kissed the tip, then the foreskin, then the shaft. Dante closed his eyes and leaned back his head. I curled my tongue around his shaft, then flicked it on his dickhead, then licked all the way to the base of his shaft. The tip of my tongue brushed against his balls.

I looked up at him. "This tastes better than tapas."

"Tapas can wait." He grinned.

I couldn't resist kissing the rest of him. I stood up from the bed and kissed up from his dick to his tight abs, to his chest, to his neck. I kissed his lips again while holding tight onto his cock.

We stood chest-to-chest and kissed tongue-on-tongue, frantically. I grabbed his ass as I licked all over his teeth and sucked on his lips.

I leaned down and put my face to his chest. I slurped at his nipple. He gasped and grabbed my head. I sucked on his nipple harder. He moaned, loudly. "Oh fuck."

"Yeah?" I let go of his nipple, then softly licked up and down his chest. "I've never had tapas like this."

"No woman ever—" He was speaking breathlessly. I went back to slurping his nipple. He pushed his chest into my mouth.

His dick was long and hard enough to be planted right on my thigh. I ran my hands up and down his naked back, his sides, his thighs, his arms: cool, pale skin, fresh from a shower.

I sat back down. I cupped his balls in my right hand. "Has a woman ever done this?"

"Yeah." He laughed through his soft moans. "But not like you do it."

"I'm a connoisseur." I pursed my lips so they would feel tighter for Dante's dick. I pulled his veiny shaft toward my mouth. He moaned as his cockhead slid through my lips, then again as his whole length entered my mouth.

I flicked my tongue on his dickhead. His precum tasted sweet, almost virginal. I scooped my tongue around the crown of his tip. Dante gasped and grabbed onto my neck. His sudden grab was like a choke hold. He was just excited.

"Fuck." Between quick breaths, he glanced down at me. His face was flushed. Beads of sweat formed on his forehead. "Nobody. Nobody's ever. Fuck. That feels so good."

I bobbed my head up and down on the length of his dick. I cupped his balls and gave them a squeeze. He squealed in response and shook his head. "Tickles!"

I looked up at his crystal blue-green eyes. They blinked every time I flicked my tongue on his cockhead. I pulled his cock out of my mouth just long enough so I could ask him: "Is this really your first time with a dude?"

"God. Yes." He palmed my scalp. "Why?"

"Well." I looked up at him. "You seem to be an expert at getting your dick sucked." I pulled it into my mouth, making sure to run my lips over the dickhead as it slid into me. I sucked and slurped again. My tongue traced every vein on his rock-hard dick.

"So if you're gay, you like—" He stared down at me again. "You enjoy fucking dudes in the ass?"

"I'm a connoisseur." I laughed. "It's your first time. I won't pressure you into anything." I shoved his dick in my mouth again and sucked on it hard. His cockhead roamed the crevices in the back of my throat.

He shut his eyes, hard. He leaned his head back. After a few seconds, he opened his eyes and looked down at me again. "I want you in my ass though."

I sucked him harder. Whether or not it was going to happen, his asking for it was fucking hot. I reached around his freshly washed ass and probed my finger at his rim. I slid his dick out of my mouth and looked up at him. "How's that?"

"Not big enough." He laughed. "I want your dick."

I sucked him harder and pumped my finger in and out of his butthole. He was pushing his ass back onto my finger and grinding up against it. Maybe he really could take my dick.

"My dick wants you." I scraped my finger up and down his assrim. "But it's gonna hurt, first time in your ass. I can't avoid that." I licked the space between his ballsack and his shaft. "I don't want you having a bad first experience in Gayworld."

"I need it in my ass." His words were breathy. His face dripped sweat. He pulled out and thrust into my mouth, fucking my lips.

I slid his dick out of my mouth, with one last little suck for his cockhead. I tongued his balls and sucked on them both, then one at a time. I looked up at his eyes, brilliant blue-green. He clenched his ass cheeks around my finger; he was begging for my dick.

I looked up at him and smiled. "I need to get the lube from my bedroom."

"Are we going to repair a bicycle?" His face broke into a laugh.

I got up, opened the door, and jogged to my bedroom. I kept a bottle of lube in the nightstand, just in case fortune smiled down at me. This one had sat unopened for five years. I took the bottle like a thief, averted my eyes from a very curious Duchess, and ran back to Dante's room.

I held the bottle up to him like I'd just received a trophy.

"I don't care about that bottle. I want your dick." He tugged at the waistband of my shorts, then slid his hand under. He half-closed his eyes while fondling my cock and balls.

I slid my shorts and underwear down. My dick popped out, against his naked thigh. I nodded at it. "Whoomp, There It Is."

He squinted like he was trying to remember something. "Tag Team. Nineteen Ninety Three. Number Two on the Billboard pop charts. Any questions?"

"You know a lot more about music than I expected." I kissed Dante's nose, his chin, his forehead, his earlobe: everywhere I hadn't yet kissed. I struggled to open the sealed lube bottle, then squeezed the clear gel all over my cock. "I'm still not convinced you can take my dick."

He took the lube bottle from me and squeezed two globs into his hands. "I've been planning for this since we kissed." He reached behind and spread lube all over his rim and hole.

I whispered: "I've been the one even scared to think about it." I always knew not to expect too much from life, to take every small pleasure as a momentary gift that wouldn't, couldn't last—

Dante dropped to his knees in front of me. Tongue first, he licked my shaft, then took it all in his mouth. My dick went from *hard* to *diamond-cutter*. He slapped my ass cheek, one and then the other. He looked up at me. "Convinced now?" He didn't wait for an answer; he stood back up, turned his lubed ass to me, and braced his arms on the wooden cabinet standing up against the wall.

I stared at the beautiful man waiting for me to take his ass. When I was nervous I always laughed. So I laughed.

Dante's face turned serious and urging. "Fuck me."

"Well that escalated quickly."

"It did." Dante looked back over his shoulder. "Now fucking pound it." He held his ass up higher, then higher still.

"Are you twerking?"

"Maybe." He laughed. "Now fuck me."

"Wait." I looked down at my bare dick. "I need a chapeau."

"A what?"

I said it a little louder: "A chapeau."

"What?"

"You know, a bedroom fedora." I made a motion of sliding an invisible condom onto my visible dick.

"A bedroom fedora?" Dante was laughing. "You call it a bedroom fedora?"

"Or a ten-gallon beanie." I shrugged, managing to keep my face deadpan straight.

"You mean a condom, right?"

"Such a vulgar word." I sighed and reached down to my wallet. My reliable pocket condom was still there. I flashed it to Dante like a police badge.

"You've always got a condom on you, huh?" Dante nodded, like he approved of my sexual mores or lack thereof.

"Hope springs eternal." I shrugged. "And you, mister famous pop star — I assume wherever you go, you haul a trailer of condoms behind you?"

"Nope. No trailer of condoms." Dante sighed. "I was never a very horny dude. Until now."

"Shit." I reached forward and ran my fingers down the length of his veiny cock, base to tip. He was rock hard. He'd been rock hard, and totally horny, during our entire encounter. "Well that's quite a change. I guess that means you're—"

"Hey." Dante shook his head.

That cut me off before I could say the *g* word.

"Less color commentary please and more dick in my ass, ok?" He was laughing. "Put on your chapeau and let's go!"

I stepped back into position behind Dante and pulled the condom onto my erect dick. I made a perfect shot of the wrapper into the trash bin.

"Three points." Dante smiled at me.

"Just wait until I slam-dunk in your ass."

"Oh, Ted!" Dante put on a ridiculous high-pitched voice. "I love it when you talk basketball!"

I gave one of his ass cheeks a good slap, then the other one. I admired its spreading redness. The twin globes of his ass were all pale, soft, freshly-showered skin and blond peach fuzz. I grabbed both his ass cheeks again, just to feel them, just to enjoy the delicious man-flesh I'd soon be penetrating.

"I'll start really slowly." I laid the length of my shaft up along his assrim. My balls just touched where his ass cheeks met his thighs. My shaft comfortably rose up along his rim.

Dante glanced back at me. "My butthole's not in my spine."

"Oh yeah, oops, I forgot." I took my dick out of the crevice between his cheeks. I started probing his butthole with my two fingers, then followed with the tip of my condomed dick. I was barely pushing the tip of my dick into his hole. "How's that? Just stop me if I'm hurting you."

"No pain. Keep going." He moved his ass up and down, inviting me deeper inside.

"It's your first time getting it in your ass. Gotta go slowly." I pushed in just a little more. For all my joking about pounding virgin ass, I certainly didn't want to cause Dante any pain.

"Still no pain." Dante bent farther over the top of the cabinet. His back stretched out beautifully. It looked like a yoga position. He braced his elbows on the cabinet and his hands against the wall. "You can go deeper, man. You can fuck me a lot deeper."

"How about now? Not too deep for you?" I pushed in more. Most of my shaft was inside him. I controlled my breathing: the warmth and tightness that my dick hadn't felt in years almost made me cum. His butthole was tight, but it didn't feel like I was going to hurt him. "Can I keep going in more?"

"Feels good." Dante looked at me. Then he thrust his ass backward. He almost knocked me down, but he impaled his lubed-up butthole on my dick. His ass cheeks were planted on my pubes. "Sorry. I got impatient." He laughed, then pushed back against me again. My cock slid into his warm, tight ass canal. It felt perfect: tight but not overwhelmingly tight. I was all the way inside him.

Dante moaned and quivered. His ass cheeks and back were now flushed red, the color of pure sex, instead of their normal cool pale color.

"Doing ok there?" I gave his ass a friendly hand-squeeze.

"Doing fucking great." He wiggled his ass to jerk my dick inside it.

"You're twerking again." I laughed and pushed into him hard. I reached around with my right hand and pushed and pulled on his long, uncut dick. His precum smelled like spiced honey.

"Do I have to do all the work around here?" Dante pushed back again, hard. This time he took my whole dick inside of him. He moved his ass back and forth a few times, taking me in and out of his hole.

"Whoa. I can do that too, you know." I pushed in and out. I sped up. He went right along with it. I could get a rhythm going and not worry about hurting him. "Every anal virgin I've tried before — I mean not that there were so many — not that many I mean — well, a few — anyway they didn't take it so eagerly."

"Even Honey Bay's infamous deflowerer can learn something new." He turned to smile back at me. Our eyes met. I kissed him. I pressed myself into him and rubbed my chest on his back.

I kept fucking him, faster and faster. The insides of his ass were warmer and warmer. He moaned and gritted his teeth with every one of my thrusts.

He reached behind and laid his hands on his ass cheeks, then pulled them apart. "Go deeper. Fuck my prostate."

"You've heard of that thing?" I laughed. "I thought that lesson was only covered in Gay School."

"Kate, once." He was laughing while sliding his feet apart and pulling his ass cheeks farther open. "She tried to finger me once. Didn't really succeed."

"I'm sorry to hear that." I pushed my dick hard into him. I was all the way in. I angled my dick upward to maybe, just maybe, hit his prostate when I plunged into him. "How's that? Am I near it?"

"Fuck!" It was a moan and a squeal and a sigh all at once. "Oh fuck! I think you got it."

I thrust in and out, pushing my cock up against his prostate every time. "I guess all that Gay School paid off." I reached around and jerked his cock and balls again, in rhythm with pushing my own dick into him and up against his prostate. I licked up between his shoulder blades all the way to his neck. I sucked on his ear and slurped at his ear hole.

Dante was moaning and shaking, pressing up against me. "Oh my fucking God." His hard dick dripped precum onto my hand.

I wrapped my left arm around his waist and stroked his dick with my right hand. I fucked his ass faster and faster. Dante's breaths were faster too, in rhythm with my fucking. Once every few thrusts he pushed back up against my dick, to impale himself deeper on my hard shaft. His ass cheeks pushed back on my pubes.

I grabbed his balls and squeezed them, then pressed my finger up onto his prostate from his ballsack. I was pressing up from the outside against the same spot I was fucking with my dick from the inside.

Dante roared. "Oh fuck!" His body was fire hot. His thighs and ass spasmed, like he was fucking the cabinet, and my hand that held his dick. I palmed his cockhead, running my fingers back and forth across it. I knew I'd catch his explosion in my hand.

A gob of cum shot out his dick, onto my hand. The smell of fresh cum filled the room. His load was huge, enough to fill my hand. "Congratulations. You're adequately hydrated." I laughed. He only moaned.

He twerked again: he lifted his ass and wiggled it on my dick. His tight hole clenched around my dick again. He shot another warm rope of cum into my hand, spilling out onto the floor.

I jerked his dick faster. I was milking him. He shot another rope of cum, then another. When he looked back at me over his shoulder, I lifted my hand to my mouth and licked a mouthful of cum off of it. It tasted like pure sex, salty and sticky and warm.

The heat coursed through me. I was getting close to cumming too. My dick and balls tingled. My thighs took on a life of their own, pumping and thrusting into him. I pushed hard into him and shot my first rope of cum into the condom.

He clenched his ass on my dick in return. He was milking me too. I moaned and shot cum again, then again. He moaned.

"Your dick's throbbing in me." He breathed hard. "Feels amazing." I embraced him from behind and kissed along his shoulder blades, then his neck, then as much of his jaw as I could reach from behind.

"Better than tapas?" I looked over at the still untouched desk of food.

"Don't know. Never had tapas before." He laughed and shook his head. My cock was slowly softening, but I left it inside him. I ran my hands up and down his abs, his taut torso, his chest, up to his shoulders.

I carefully pulled out of his ass. He stood up and turned around in the same motion and kissed me, staring into my eyes.

"Hold on." I pulled off my very full condom and tossed it in the garbage. "Sombrero disposal."

"Give a hoot, don't pollute." He shrugged and kissed me again. Sweat dripped from his face onto mine.

I laid my hands on his ass cheeks. I could feel their heat even before my hands made contact. "We're gonna eat those tapas, right?"

"Well somebody's hungry." He pulled out a chair and put it in front of the desk. "Have a seat."

"I did do all the work just now." I wiped sweat from my forehead.

"What?!" He shook his head.

"Just kidding." I sighed. He'd been fucking my dick just as hard as I'd been fucking his ass. "Go to Google sometime and look up *power bottom*. That's you."

"I think I can imagine what it means without going to Gay School." He opened the lid on one styrofoam box. Sliced olives and parmesan on bruschetta. "Open wide!"

I opened my mouth. He slid the bread in. "What can I bring you to drink?"

"Oh shit. I forgot to buy sangria with the tapas." I shook my head. "Grab whatever from the refrigerator I guess?"

"Sure." He started to get up.

"Are you really feeding me, Dante? Nobody's done anything like that for me."

"Yes." He nodded enthusiastically. "You've been — you've been so nice to me." He started toward the door. "You think it's ok with the landlord if I run around the house naked?"

"You already jizzed on the cabinet." I shrugged and looked over the drops of his sticky white cum on the cabinet he'd been bending over. "Might as well break all the rules."

He waved and laughed, then jogged out the door. His glutes flexed and pumped as he ran out. I still felt every ridge and turn of his ass canal on my dick.

He ran down the stairs. I heard him opening the refrigerator and the cabinets. Then he ran back up. "You're all out of drinks!"

I sighed. "No, *we're* all out of drinks."

"Alright, *we're* all out of drinks." He picked up a fried meatball with a plastic spoon and moved it toward my mouth. "Brrr! Whizzzz! Meatball coming in for a landing!"

"Darling, you know I don't eat balls before dinnertime." I pursed my lips and shook my head.

"Oh yes you do." He shook his hips a little. Just fucking adorable.

"Oh yeah. I do eat balls before dinnertime." I shrugged and opened wide. He loaded the meatball into my mouth. "How can I say no when you shove your balls in my piehole?"

"In your what?"

"Never mind." I leaned in and kissed him. I ran my hands all over his slim, tight torso. I sat him down and looked in his eyes. "I'd rather be kissing your piehole."

"After fucking my cornhole?" He raised his eyebrows at me.

"Yeah pretty much."

"Speaking of pie. And corn. We need to go buy drinks and groceries, don't we?" He glanced out the door and down the stairs. "I think I ate and drank everything you had."

"Yeah, I guess we do." I whispered in his ear. "By the way, I've never been *we* until today. Not with anybody."

He pecked my cheek. "I've never had a dick in my cornhole until today." He shrugged and laughed. "I guess we're even."

6

Dante

"Always stay at the store's outer edges." Ted spoke to me conspiratorially, leaning in and almost whispering. Meanwhile, he did that same grandiose hand-sweep, as if the grocery store were nothing more than a tiny part of his vast empire. "The good things, the fresh things, the gourmet things, are at the outer edges."

"And what's in the interior?" I tried to sound apprehensive. Ted's lectures were adorable.

"There be dragons!" Ted was almost shouting up at the store's tiled ceiling. "Fritos. Cheetos. Doritos. Tostitos." He scrunched up his nose and shook his head.

"Man, you don't like Cheetos?" I scrunched my nose and shook my head.

"Dante Huxley." Ted squinted into my eyes. "If you consume highly processed hydrogenated oil quote-unquote snack foods that are delivery mechanisms for three times your daily allowance of salt and sugar—"

"I'm just playing with you." I laughed at him. In his face. Playfully. "I don't even like Cheetos."

"Promise?" Ted stared at me with maybe the most serious face I'd ever seen on him. "You have to promise."

"Promise." I gently clapped his back. Solid. Beefy. I'd probably have a build like that when I was Ted's age. "No Fritos or Doritos or Tostitos either."

I started checking out the tomato selection. I hadn't seen an actual grocery store in years.

"Not even Tostitos? Double-dog promise?" Ted held up a curled pinky finger. I curled my own pinky around his and gave him a quick kiss on the lips.

"Is that Ted Baker?" someone asked from around the stack of tomato crates. "Ted Baker buys tomatoes at Publix?"

Ted called back at the mysterious voice. "What's wrong with buying tomatoes at Publix?"

A man emerged from around the corner: tall, wiry, with floppy hair falling over his eyes. "I always thought Ted Baker would have his tomatoes flown in from private heirloom greenhouses in France, his milk from free-range, free-thinker, free-love cows free-grazing only on fine organic grass—"

"Ah, what the heart desires, but the wallet forbids!" Ted shook his wallet at the man. "Andy. Baxter. How are you gentlemen?"

"Pretty good, considering the store is all out of key lime pie." The wiry man extended his hand to me. "Hey, I'm Andy. That's my husband Baxter."

"Hi." I shook Andy's hand. "I'm Dante Huxley."

Baxter nodded at me. "You do look a lot like Dante Huxley. You could play weddings or something."

"Except I'm the real Dante Huxley. Not an imitator." I shrugged. "The only thing worse than getting recognized as a celebrity is getting mistaken for an imposter."

"No way." Baxter stepped back and looked at me. "You're seriously Dante Huxley? Super pop star Dante Huxley?"

Andy grinned at Baxter. "If he's Dante Huxley, then I'm Reza Pahlavi." Baxter rolled his eyes.

"What?" Ted shook his head at the two of them.

"Reza Pahlavi was the Shah of Iran." Baxter said it with a sigh. "I'm married to Andy. I already got used to his brand of humor."

"Ok, I'm not the Shah of Iran. And I know that Dante Huxley is supposed to be in town." Andy stared at my face up-close like he was trying to judge a counterfeit dollar bill. "But *you*? Really? You're Dante Huxley? Just right here, standing right in front of me?"

"Me, really. I'm Dante Huxley." I put my arm around Ted. "And this is Ted, my— well— my temporary landlord. And friend."

"Ted Baker is hanging out with Dante Huxley?" Andy roared with laughter, then quickly covered his mouth with his hand. "Dante Huxley from the boy band Inferno? Ted Baker from Deep Down Music?"

"Shh." Ted play-punched Andy. "We're adhering to a ceasefire about music."

"Holy shit," Andy mouthed silently. "Ted Baker. Dante Huxley. Together."

"Hey." Baxter squeezed Andy's hand. "Do you guys want to come over for dinner today? I'm making spaghetti." With his other hand he palmed a tomato.

"Spaghetti dinner scales up quite economically. It would cost us no more than five dollars to make additional spaghetti for the two of you." Andy laughed like a nerd from old movies about high school nerds. "So it's a good night for us to invite you over for dinner."

"Dante?" Ted smiled at me. "What do you think? You wanna hang with Andy and Baxter for dinner? They're pretty cool guys."

"Sure." I nodded and gave a thumbs-up. "I've been pretty much a recluse since I got to Honey Bay. Would be nice to hang out with people. People who don't even think I'm famous." I smiled at Andy.

Andy started laughing again, covering his mouth. "What kind of Airbnb algorithm sent you to live with the town music snob?" He was shaking his head and looking at me and Ted.

"Hey!" Ted made a motion of zipping his lips. "Dante and I have a truce. No discussions of his music."

I shrugged at him. "Ok, boomer. Call it a truce."

Ted took a deep breath. "Boomer? I am barely in my thirties—"

"Just getting you all wound up again." I laughed.

"That's how this Dante guy operates. He knows how to push my buttons." Ted shook his head at me, then looked over at Andy. Andy looked like the kind of guy who was smart enough to catch the double meaning. "So guys, let's meet in half an hour at that vulgar McMansion you guys built on the old mini-golf course?"

"Yeah!" Andy nodded, enthusiastically enough for his floppy hair to flap like a flag. "Meet at our place!"

"You forgot to mention, Teddy." Baxter grinned at Ted. "That house was built with dirty Rawlins Telecom money. As you always call it, *the vulgar McMansion built with dirty money*. I'm disappointed in you for not mentioning it this time!"

"I was kind of saving that point for dinner conversation. Where I drag you over the coals for being a one-percenter." Ted shrugged. "And don't call me *Teddy*."

"Good man. I'm looking forward to your outrage." Baxter nodded. "And I'll call you Teddy anytime I want."

Ted sent a huge grimace Baxter's way. I took Ted's hand and led him toward the wine aisle, as if to lead him away from a brawl.

Driving us to dinner, Ted recited a rapid-fire history of Andy and Baxter. High school sweethearts from Honey Bay, reunited after ten years apart. Andy now hosted a radio show. Baxter was the scion of the Rawlins Telecom empire. Ted sometimes showed up on Andy's radio show to give his opinions on music and generally kvetch about things.

"Well, there's the McMansion." Ted pointed and shook his head as he pulled into the driveway, behind a blue Lamborghini. "Their house is vulgar and ostentatious and disgusting and I love it and desperately wish I could afford a living space just like it."

It looked like an airport terminal, with brilliant white walls and floor-to-ceiling glass. Behind it were the remnants of a mini-golf course: castle, windmill, and all. Despite all his mockery of it, Ted looked at the whole house as if it were a holy site.

The front door was open. Lights were on inside. Ted knocked on it anyway. "Hey! Somebody parked a Lamborghini in front of your house! I already called the tow truck."

"Yeah, yeah," Baxter called out from inside. "Come in. Admire our McMansion. Or make fun of it."

Ted walked in. I followed. The house looked like the celebrity mansions that were always being pushed in front of me. I'd never even had enough time off from touring to consider those houses seriously. But this house was nice. Really nice.

Ted nodded approvingly at Andy and Baxter standing over the kitchen counter. "Guys. This kitchen is the size of my entire house."

A mischievous grin crossed Baxter's face as he sliced tomatoes. "Andy is a size queen." Baxter elbow-bumped Andy, then glanced back at Ted.

Andy muttered loudly through his closed mouth: "If I were a size queen, I wouldn't be with you."

"Hey now!" Ted called out. "Enough with the fisticuffs. Do you guys need any help preparing the pasta?"

"Sure." Baxter cleared his throat. "Ted, would you mind passing me another can of SpaghettiOs? And a jar of Ragu."

Ted's face turned to alarm for a full second, until he laughed. "I'm not gonna fall for that. You guys know me too well."

Baxter turned to me. "So Dante, how is it putting up with Florida Man?"

I clicked my tongue at Baxter. "Aren't you a Florida man yourself?"

"Ok, you got me." Baxter sighed. "But I'm not crazy like Ted. How's it putting up with Ted's brand of crazy?"

"I'm not really putting up with anything." I shrugged and absentmindedly started peeling a clove of garlic. "I mean, Ted is my landlord. We stay out of each other's way for the most part."

Maybe that was a little harsh. But it was true.

"The way you guys were grocery-shopping together," Andy grinned and moved his floppy hair off of his eyes, "you looked like a happy couple."

"Ah yeah." Baxter cleared his throat loudly and sent Andy a look. "Andy, wanna help me put the spaghetti in boiling water over here?"

"Oops." Andy's face turned red. "Speaking of boiling water."

"It's fine." Ted sighed. "Dante and I both aren't the easiest personalities in the world. I think that's one thing we can agree on."

"Bingo!" I snapped my fingers in the air. "What Florida man said."

"Sit down, guys." Baxter showed us to the dining room.

"You didn't do that Ted hand-wave," I said to Baxter. "That grandiose wave Ted does when he shows you a room of his house or something."

"Oh, this." Baxter perfectly imitated the Ted hand-wave. He repeated it a few times, like a film loop. "Behold, my forests, my meadows, my horse stables, my lands!"

Ted burst out laughing. "Baxter, shouldn't you be cooking? You've got a dinner to make."

"Yeah get back in here!" Andy yelled out, amid the sounds of a running sink and banging pans. "Like my mom always taught me: a man's place is in the kitchen."

Baxter shook his head. "I have to do all the work around here."

Andy called out from the kitchen: "*Almost* all the work, Baxter." His tone of voice sounded like he wasn't talking about the kitchen. "*Almost* all the work."

"Hey now." Ted waved his hands in front of his face. "I listen to Andy on WHON. I don't need to listen to TMI."

"WHON?" I asked Ted. "That's the local radio station that you mentioned?"

"Ah, WHON!" Ted said. "Yes, most definitely. We do have a fine local radio station in Honey Bay. Andy is the superstar DJ and chat host, and Baxter is in charge of the business side and sleeping on the job after a big sushi lunch."

"I heard that!" Baxter shouted from the kitchen.

"So Andy is that DJ who blabbed on the radio that I'm in Honey Bay?" I said it a little bit loudly. If Andy and Baxter were teasing Ted, I could tease them right back.

"I believe so, yes." Ted cleared his throat. "I think Andy's trying to make it up to you with a free plate of spaghetti."

"As a radio professional," Andy said from the kitchen, "I always maintain good relations with the celebrity world."

Ted shouted toward the kitchen: "Is that a nice way of saying you're a starfucker?"

"Be nice!" Baxter peeked out at us from the kitchen. "Or I'll cum in everyone's spaghetti."

"Four plates?" Ted shook his head. "You're not eighteen anymore, buckaroo."

"Wanna see me try?" Baxter didn't sound like he was joking.

"Um, how about *no*?" I yelled toward the kitchen. "I'd be interested in hearing more about Andy's radio show instead."

"Hmm. You can appear on the show if you want." Andy's voice echoed from the kitchen. "If Baxter's spaghetti doesn't kill you tonight, I can interview you on the show tomorrow."

"Nah." I sighed.

"No confidence in my spaghetti?" Baxter walked out of the kitchen with two bowls of spaghetti for me and Ted. He set them down in front of us.

"This spaghetti smells amazing. I wouldn't even know that you shot your load into it." I sniffed the two bowls and gave Baxter a thumbs-up. "About being on Andy's show, it's more like I've got nothing to talk about, I guess."

Andy and Baxter came out of the kitchen with their own two bowls of spaghetti. Everything smelled like comfortable home cooking, the kind I hadn't had in the years since I hit it big. The four of us presided over their dining table that was proportioned for a dozen or two guests.

It was difficult not to think of the four of us as two couples: Andy and Baxter, Ted and Dante. I had to remind myself that Ted and I weren't a couple. Not quite.

Whatever Ted and I were, we were. If not a couple, then at least a *we*.

"I can't believe I have to actually tell you, a pop star, to do this." Andy laughed. "But how about doing what any pop star does when appearing on a radio show: promoting your newest album?"

"You know that Inferno broke up, right?" I shoved a forkful of spaghetti in my mouth.

"Yeah, so?" Andy passed me and Ted two glasses of red wine. "You still get paid the royalties."

Ted held his wine glass up in the air. "As Dante's landlord, I propose a toast to royalties." The four of us toasted.

"I do get royalties." I swallowed a gulp of red wine. "Roland does too. He co-wrote all the songs with me. Back when we were on speaking terms."

"Oh, Roland is the guy who—" Andy started to say. "Yeah, Roland. I remember reading the story. We won't bring it up on the show. Just promote your albums. I'll give you some softball interview questions. Your favorite food, stuff like that."

"Tapas." I smiled at Ted. "Definitely tapas."

Baxter cleared his throat. "I have a feeling that Dante is now the one broadcasting on the TMI frequency."

"Dante and I eat tapas when we, when we—" Ted looked at me, like he didn't know how to finish his sentence.

I piped up: "When we wax the floors!" I nodded as believably as I could.

"Alright." Baxter shook his head. "We don't need to hear the details of how you guys, uh, wax the floors."

"Can we get back to business here?" Andy tapped a spoon on the edge of his plate, like a call to order. It was delightfully juvenile. "I'm trying to get world-famous pop star Dante Huxley on my radio show, and you guys can think of nothing better to discuss than waxing floors."

"Alright." I tapped my fork on the plate as a callback to Andy. "I'll be on your show tomorrow. I'm sure I'll be able to come up with something to say."

"Better carb-load tonight!" Andy pointed at the bowl of spaghetti in front of me. "The banter on my show gets pretty intense!"

"If I can survive dinner with you guys—" I smiled at Baxter, then at Andy. They really were a lot of fun. "Then I can definitely survive anything."

Ted raised his hand to speak between mouthfuls of spaghetti. "Even sharing a house with Florida Man."

"Even that." I gave Ted a thumbs-up.

The rest of the night was a blur of pasta, wine, and Baxter and Andy quibbling over the details of the stories they told about themselves. They made couplehood seem enjoyable. Not just something done for the cameras. And not absolutely terrifying.

The next day, I arrived at the station fifteen minutes before the start of my noon interview. I wasn't a very busy guy anyway.

Exactly, Andy introduced me as Dante Huxley. He played a clip of one of Inferno's hit songs: me and Roland wailing away in unison about lost love.

Andy was brilliant with his words: "So my understanding, Dante, is that you are no longer in the band Inferno? Am I correct?"

He lobbed that pitch to me so perfectly that I could've hit a homerun even if I hadn't been practicing for the interview on the walk over to the station. I could promote our back catalog without being Roland's bitch. And I could mention my own solo career without having to explain myself.

"That is correct. I'm not in the band anymore. But Inferno has some great albums. Our most recent album, *Fire*, well, it really is fire."

"Indeed!" Andy nodded. "I highly recommend Inferno's newest album, *Fire*. It goes a lot deeper than the single that everybody knows, 'That's How I Shake It.'"

I nodded. "The album is of course available online, and at most music stores. Most." I wasn't going to send the listeners to Ted's store for him to yell them out of the shop. But I also wasn't going to send them to Ted's competitors.

"*Most* music stores." Andy smiled an inside-joke acknowledgment in my direction, and he left it at that. We weren't going to mock our friend Ted. Not overtly, anyway. Andy cleared his throat and continued: "So what's on your plate musically now, Dante? What does the future hold?"

"I think I've matured a lot since I first started Inferno. I want to try some solo work. You know, Inferno was a wonderful experience, but I'm starting to work on a new solo album."

"That's exciting. That's really exciting." Andy smiled at me. "Can I ask you just one more question, Dante?"

I spoke clearly into the microphone: "Briefs."

Andy laughed. His face flushed red. "Not that question. That was totally unscripted, by the way, ladies and gentlemen. Live radio." Andy actually turned red. "But my question is, how do you like Honey Bay?"

"I love Honey Bay."

My answer was perfectly honest. I loved Honey Bay.

CHERISH HIM

I was even falling in love with my terrible landlord. After the radio interview, I dropped in on him at his store. Hoodie up. Not that it helped much.

"We just heard you on the radio!" Ted's assistant shouted out to me as soon as I stepped in.

"I thought I was in stealth mode." I dropped down my hoodie. It was hopeless.

Ted was giving me a double thumbs-up from behind his counter. "You and Andy both sounded great on the interview."

"Wow, you listened. Even though I'm just a stupid pop star."

"Hey, we have a truce, remember?" Ted cleared his throat. "Nice marketing work too. We've sold five Inferno CDs just in the half hour since your interview aired."

"Here at Deep Down? You sold Inferno CDs here?" I almost wanted to step outside and make sure I was in the right store.

"Uh—" Ted looked down at his hands.

"Lookee here!" His assistant stood in front of an endcap full of Inferno CDs. "He just got these CDs in on special order yesterday."

"I mean—" Ted shook his head. "Business is business. Since you showed up in town, everybody's been asking for Inferno albums. I kind of had to—"

"Ted's still pretty salty about it," his assistant called out. "We've sold more product today than we did all last month."

Ted sighed loudly. "Sometimes, Angelica, even a patrician has to abide by the instincts of the masses."

Angelica mock-whispered to me: "I caught him dancing to 'That's How I Shake It' in his office."

Ted rolled his eyes at Angelica. "Sounds like somebody's been watching the security camera feed when she should've been alphabetizing albums."

"Ted was dancing?" I looked at Angelica, then over at Ted.

Ted looked back at me. He laid down his barcode scanner and raised his hands to shoulder height. Eyes fixed on me, shook his ass left and right. Then left and right again.

Angelica laughed. I tried to restrain myself, but laughed twice as hard as she did.

Ted nodded at the two of us. He smiled at me. "That's how I shake it."

7

Ted

"This is really cozy." Dante's breath smelled like toothpaste, his hair like Pantene. He nuzzled his face into the crook of my shoulder, the way Duchess had done the first evening I took her home from the shelter. Dante's warm breath brushed against my chest.

"Yes it is." I kissed his forehead. With his big toe, he traced the outline of my foot. "We don't get blizzards in Florida, but this is the closest thing."

Torrential rain pounded outside the window. The sheets of water coming down reflected what little moonlight could sneak through cloud cover. Duchess lay on my desk and meowed at the howling wind.

"I think I can hear the waves crashing." Dante looked up at me with brilliant green eyes. "I usually can't hear the waves from here."

"Yeah, we're only three blocks away." I glanced out the window. I could sometimes catch a glimpse of ocean, at least during the day, when the trees swayed just right. "The seawall's getting its ass pounded."

Dante laughed while looking up at my face. "Is that the official update from weather dot gay?" He kissed my neck.

I nodded. "Ass-pounding waves, gobs of warm liquid sprayed all over us, and a lot of blowing."

"Glad I'm comfy in your arms then." Dante licked my nipple. My dick responded instantly and tented the sheets.

Dante pointed at the sheet tented over my dick. "Is that a rising storm?" He reached down and caressed my cockhead and shaft through the sheet.

Another gust of wind howled. Tree branches outside the window went flying down onto the ground. Duchess jumped off the desk and hid under the bed.

Then a big crash. Somewhere else in the house. It sounded like a wrecking ball had come through, followed by howls of wind.

I got up and put my phone into flashlight mode. Dante got up behind me. Once we opened my bedroom door, the open-window sound was obviously coming from Dante's room. It sounded like an open car window on the highway.

Dante opened the door to his room. Three corners of the room were alright. The fourth corner, farthest from the door, had been replaced by a large tree branch. The tree branch looked like it had just taken a bite out of the corner of the house. Wind and rain poured in from the opening.

I grabbed Dante's laptop and his guitar and carried them to the walk-in closet in the hallway. Wordlessly, Dante started doing the same with his other belongings. The rain and wind had destroyed only a bit of my house and furniture, none of Dante's belongings.

"Shit, your house." Dante looked at the hole in the room with terror.

"Did we move out all your stuff? You got any more socks or underwear or something around? Because it'll all get drenched by the rain."

"Yeah, we got everything." Dante looked down the hallway at the pile of his belongings in the walk-in closet. The wind howled through the room. "But what about your house? That corner of the room is destroyed."

"You've never been a Florida homeowner, have you?" I grinned at Dante and led him outside the ruined room, then closed the door firmly behind us.

"Um, no, I haven't. And you've never played a show at Wembley Stadium, have you?"

"No, I haven't." I laughed. "Anyway, that's why we have insurance. A bit of inconvenience, but insurance will cover repairs. Even pays for the loss of use of the living space. So it's fine. It'll all be fixed."

"Oh." Dante smiled.

I led him back to my room. "Your room, obviously, is not going to be usable in the interim. I can't imagine that repair taking less than a month."

"Oh." Dante glanced back toward his room longingly, like a kitten taken from his favorite resting spot.

"I can give you a refund if you want. It hasn't even been one month yet since you moved in. You can find another place to stay. I can go to the bank in the morning and get the cash and refund you. Don't worry about Airbnb."

"Mmm." Dante was still looking at me, then my room, then the door to his room.

"Or you can move into my room with me." I held up my arms like I was offering a last resort. In a way I was. "Which I realize is not easy. I've never shared a room either. I've never even had a boyfriend."

"You haven't?" Dante laughed.

"Is the wind outside impairing your hearing?" I laughed. "I'm no virgin, but I've never had a long-term relationship. I mean not until—" I stopped myself and waited for Dante.

Dante opened his eyes wide. He was still looking back-and-forth between his room and mine. He took a half-step out of my room and looked one more time at his things in the walk-in closet. "I'll move into your room, Ted. Should be fine. I'm in your room more and more anyway."

He breathed in deeply, like he was preparing for something big, and smiled at me. Those same brilliantly white teeth of his I'd considered pop-star overkill when I'd first met him, were now the most beautiful I'd ever seen.

I kissed him. "Dante. I'll try. I'll really try not to be a jerk."

He wrapped his arms around me and ran them up and down my sides, like he was warming me up against the rainstorm. He pressed his face to mine and kissed me, hard. Then he whispered into my ear: "I'm not in the best shape emotionally. I lost my fiancée. I lost my band. But I'll try. I'll try to be good. I'll try to make it work."

Dante slurped on my lips, then drew away and stared into my eyes. Outside, the wind still howled.

His tongue drew a line down along my shoulder blade, until he kissed my pecs and sucked one nipple, then the other. I spoke between quick breaths. "Did I teach you how delicious man-nipples are?"

"Maybe." He smiled up at me. Kissing down from my chest to my stomach, he squatted down, then knelt. My hard dick lay in his palm. "You know how I'm better than this rainstorm?"

He looked up at me like he really wanted an answer. I looked at him like I really wanted a blowjob.

"How are you better than this rainstorm?"

"I can keep blowing all night, and then some." He plunged the entirety of my dick into his mouth. Its warmth was exactly what I needed. His tongue danced around the crown of my dickhead. Maybe he'd learned that from me too.

He took my dick out of his mouth and stared at it up-close in the dim light. "I've actually never seen one close-up." He ran his eyes over it from tip to base, then followed the same path with his tongue. "Having one isn't the same as seeing one close-up."

"Unless you're a dog."

"Yeah, unless you're a dog." He puckered his lips and drenched my shaft in small kisses, then tongued and sucked on my balls.

"You know, I'm seriously not accustomed to this level of oral stimulation." I watched his beautiful blond hair, messy from bed, not upstyled, as he slid my cock in and out of his mouth. He gave it an extra slurp and an extra tongue-kiss at every insertion.

"Is that your fancy way of saying you might cum soon?" He looked up at me again. He held my dick up to his eyes almost like it was a blindfold.

"Yes it is. You're quite the cocksmith."

"Cocksmith?" He laughed.

"Yeah. You know. The way you work my cock." I ran my hands through his hair.

He sucked it deep into his mouth, until my tip was in his throat. Then he hummed and looked up straight at me. I had to clench my jaw and grit my teeth to stop myself from cumming.

He let my dick out of his mouth and caught it in his hand. Still cradling my dick in his hand, he stood up. He held his palm up to my chest. He pushed me down onto the bed. I gasped. Nobody had ever done that.

His eyes fixed on mine, he licked from my taint, to my balls, all the way to the tip of my dick. He slurped at the tip of my cock, then looked at me again. "I'm gonna take your ass."

"You're gonna what?" I laughed. He was talking like an expert. "I knew you're a cocksmith. I didn't know you're also an ass-wrangler."

"Raise your legs up." He smacked my ass cheek. I raised my legs high up and parted them. I didn't know what was going to happen, but I was willing to play along — whatever he wanted to try out, I was likely to have already done more than a few times with whatever Grindr flesh had been passing through town.

He kissed up from my ass cheeks to my calves, then my ankles, then my feet. "Wait. Hold on." He sounded impatient. He got up and jogged to the walk-in closet that held his things, then came back. "Just needed these."

He held baby wipes in one hand, a condom in the other. He pinned my legs back and feasted on my balls, sucking on them, then manhandling them between his palms and fingers, and kneading them with his two hands. Then he took a few baby wipes and gave my asshole a generous cleaning.

I nodded at him approvingly. "Were you valedictorian at gay school?" He quickly rolled the condom on his dick, then grabbed the lube from my nightstand.

"I was only salutatorian," he whispered. "I'll be valedictorian once I've fucked your ass."

"Whatever I can do to help your advancement." I held my legs up high and separated my ass cheeks. "Nice cleaning job. My rim feels like a meadow of daisies."

"Maybe it feels like a meadow of daisies." He smiled up at me. Then he dove into my ass, tongue first. He licked all the way from the top of my assrim to my taint, then to my balls. "But it still tastes like ass." He grinned.

"You mean that only in the best way, right?"

"Sure." He gave my rim another long, slow lick. This time he teased inside my butthole with his rolled-up tongue. "I'm not even sure what ass is supposed to taste like. But yours tastes great."

"Your first time at the salad bar?" I laughed. He answered by shoving his tongue deep inside my butthole. "Oh fuck!" I groaned. It wasn't my first time at the salad-tossing station, but it had been a long while since anyone's tongue had gone there. The sounds of rain and thunder outside and the howling wind in the next room made the ass-tonguing feel even more intense.

Dante licked up and down both sides of my assrim, pulled my cheeks apart, then thrust his tongue deep in. He wiggled it inside my ass and looked up at me from between my ass cheeks. He quickly pushed his tongue into my butthole then back out. He got a rhythm going.

He laid his hands under my ass cheeks and squeezed on my ass in rhythm with tongue-fucking my butthole. His hot breath tickled my rim.

"If I lay a finger on my own dick now, I'll cum."

"Is that a warning?" Dante asked between licks of my hole.

"Yeah." I played with his ears as he ate me out. "Hurry up and just fuck my ass."

"You sure you can take it?" He grinned. "I'm pretty big. And you seem like a top."

"I take what I can get." I laughed. "And if you can take a dick, trust me, I can take one too."

"So you ready now?" He blew a gust of breath on my rim.

"Yeah." I was laughing from the sensation. "But you're blowing on my asshole like it's a birthday cake."

Dante shrugged. "I always said birthday cake tastes like ass." He rose himself up until he was kneeling, his face at the level of my ankles and feet. He kissed my calves and ankles again, then squirted lube into my rim.

I groaned. "Feels like Wet 'N Wild down there." His saliva, plus my natural lubrication, plus a few big squirts of gel — the combination made my ass almost too well-lubricated.

"Time to slide!" Dante said with a laugh. He pushed his dick into me. It slipped into my hole without much pain. "How's that?"

"Feels fine. You're big but it doesn't hurt." I gyrated my ass up against his dick, just as he'd done for me.

"The thunderstorm outside." He brought his torso forward, then leaned down so his side came down between my thighs. He brought his face to mine. He kissed my lips. "The thunderstorm is fucking sexy." He thrust his dick deeper into me.

"It is." I laid my head back. I wanted him to ravish me with kisses. He did: he built up a rhythm fucking my ass and kissed my neck, my jaw, my ears, then my lips. He slid his tongue deep into my mouth while he fucked me.

I was breathing in rhythm with his thrusts. I pushed my ass back at his dick whenever I could manage the energy, just to pull him deeper inside me. He breathed quickly and leaned down to kiss my lips whenever he could. His sweat dropped off onto my body.

He gently slapped my ass cheek, then grabbed my dick and stared at it while smiling.

"Oh fuck," I said. "You've got your hand on the trigger." The blowjob, the rimjob, the dick in my ass, the kisses, and now this gorgeous, loving man riding on top of me as he fucked me — it was too much. If he played with my dick, I couldn't hold back.

He kept fucking me. He gripped my dick hard. "You think you can wait until I get there?"

"I want you to cum first." I pushed my ass into his dick and wrapped my legs around his waist as he fucked me.

"So I can keep fucking you hard?" He smiled down at me.

"Yeah. You can keep talking dirty too." I reached around to his ass and slapped it.

"Talking dirty?" He made an innocent face while he kept fucking me hard. "I don't know who's talking dirty here." He leaned down and kissed my lips forcefully. He shoved his tongue past my pursed lips and ran his tongue over my teeth.

He closed his eyes. He put his tongue out all the way in my mouth, like he was going to lick in my throat. He pushed deep enough into me so the tip of his cock touched my prostate. He pulled out and pushed even deeper in. I moaned and squirmed as his entire dick filled me.

He pulled out and started pumping harder and faster than I'd ever been fucked. He thrust in and out of me and sucked on my lips. We both were breathing quickly.

"How's that?" He slapped my ass cheek while he thrust in. Then he stuck his finger in alongside his dick.

That did it. I gasped and my dick throbbed. He grabbed it and jerked it fast just as it started throbbing. Cum flew up onto his chest and dripped back down onto me.

He fucked faster. Sweat ran down from his flushed red face. Even his hair was a sweaty mess. The room smelled like sweat and cum.

He looked down at me with wide-open eyes, then moaned. He thrust in with all the power of his thighs. His dick was throbbing and cumming. The condom was filling up inside my ass like a water balloon. Dante was jackhammering his dick into me as he spurted cum into his rubber.

He grabbed my dick with one hand and my ass cheek with the other as he pushed and rubbed his dick and balls hard up against my ass. "I'm fucking cumming!" He spoke through quick breaths. His body was red hot.

"I could've told you that." I laughed and took a fingerful of my cum off my chest, and put it up to his lips. He slurped the cum off my finger and closed his eyes. The last ropes of cum shot out into his condom in my ass while his dick throbbed just a few more times.

He collapsed onto me, on top of me. He reached down and pulled his dick out of my ass.

I didn't let go of him. I wrapped my arms and legs more completely around him. I inhaled all of him and kissed him hard.

8

Dante

I woke in my favorite position: my face buried somewhere in Ted's arm. I opened my eyes to the gentle curve of his tricep, in extreme close-up, like a real-life macro lens. His other arm was wrapped solidly around my torso, ending in his hand, which held his phone.

"Oh, you guys are already on it?" He was speaking into his phone. "Wonderful. I'll bring photos. I'll be right down there. Thanks so much." Ted disconnected the phone conversation.

I clicked my tongue at him. "Photos? Are you auditioning for porn?"

"What—"

"You know, you said you'd bring photos." I rolled over in maximum laziness and looked up at the ceiling. My own room's ceiling was wrecked, but what did I care, when I could stay in Ted's bed?

"Insurance company, not porn audition. Sorry to disappoint." Ted shrugged, jostling my head up a little. He kissed my forehead.

"That's exactly what an undercover porn star *would* say!" I nodded at him.

"Alright, alright, you've got me. Deep Down Music is actually a front for Deep Inside Video." Ted burst out laughing.

"I knew it!" I grabbed his semi-hard dick and nodded like a detective. "I suspected you were a little too good at buttfucking to be just a music store owner."

"And I would've gotten away with it, too!" Ted sighed. "No, seriously, we gotta go downtown. It's past noon already. Insurance company has a mobile claims center set up downtown. They're there until three."

"Oh, so that's who you were talking to." I did my best to look dejected. "That's a lot less exciting."

"They said pretty much the whole town sustained damage. No casualties, just a lot of wreckage."

I squeezed Ted's ass. "I thought it was only your anal virginity that got destroyed."

"Ain't no insurance for that." He laughed loudly. Duchess meowed and ran out from under the bed. Ted snapped some photos of the house damage, I opened a can of Whiskas for Duchess, and we were off.

Downtown, Ted parked the Range Rover in front of Deep Down Music. His store building wasn't damaged at all. In the middle of a busy street, it had been well out of the way of any falling branches. Ted checked in with Angelica while I admired the Inferno endcap display. We walked from Deep Down to the blue-and-white semi trailer with a Floridian Insurance logo.

"Alice Silver!" Ted yelled out at a slim, middle-aged woman with glasses and a ponytail. She was carrying a clipboard and directing foot traffic around the insurance claims area. "You never get tired of saving the world, do you?"

"Eh." She turned up her nose. "I do what I can. My castle wasn't damaged — the advantage of living in a castle, right? — so I'm helping out everyone here."

"Castle?" I mouthed silently at Ted.

"Oh!" Ted clapped me on the back. "Remember that mini-golf castle behind Andy and Baxter's house?"

"Vaguely." I nodded.

"Alice lives in that castle. She's Andy's mom. Operations manager of WHON. Longtime community activist." Ted beamed a smile at Alice.

"Cut it out with the *longtime* bit, Teddy." Alice shook her head at him.

"Did Baxter teach you to say that?" Ted's eyebrows rose, along with his voice.

"Teach me to say what, Teddy?" Alice held up her hands to show her innocence.

"You know full well." Ted shook his head. He looked like he was about to stomp his feet. "Anyway, how's the town doing?"

"So-so." Alice sighed. "We've got a few hundred homeless so far."

"A few hundred?" Ted stared at Alice.

"Cats and dogs. From the shelter. Shelter was pretty much destroyed." Alice pointed over somewhere down the street. "You can't even see what's left of it."

"What happened to the animals?" I asked. I imagined a few hundred cats and dogs making a temporary home at Ted's place. Not optimal, but if that was what was needed—

"Animals are fine for now." Alice waved her hand. "We've got more than enough people volunteering to foster them. We're telling them *a few months*."

"And then?"

"Good question." Alice sighed. "The shelter didn't have storm insurance. Repairs will cost about a hundred thousand. Not exactly play money. I can make some phone calls and get some donated services and materials, but it's still gonna be expensive."

"Sorry to ask the obvious." Ted raised a finger in the air. "Did you talk to the Rawlins Telecom folks?"

"Already did." Alice nodded. "Baxter talked to his dad too. They pledged five thousand and said that's the most they can do. We've been coming to them for every single thing the town needs — not quite fair to them either."

Ted leaned in to whisper to Alice: "I might be able to dig something up from the vast reserves of wealth I keep hidden under my failing music store."

"Oh? That's very kind of you, Ted." Alice patted his shoulder.

"Seriously." Ted nodded. "Put me down for a thousand bucks toward the shelter. I'm sorry I can't do more."

"Still very generous of you." Alice gave Ted the most genuine smile I'd ever seen from anyone.

Ted frowned at her. "But you have to stop calling me *Teddy*."

Alice shrugged. "I'll think about it. For now, you'd better go over to the claims processing desk and hope they don't call you *Teddy* too."

Ted frowned as he walked away. "I'm a paying customer. I will let them do no such thing." He pulled out his phone and started showing photos to the claims agent.

"Dante Huxley!" Two girls in matching red curls shouted at me. They stood in front of me side-to-side, like they were blocking my way. I was used to this kind of shit from my young fans, although I'd mercifully not seen much of it in Honey Bay.

I forced myself to smile at them. "Hey, I always appreciate my fans, but this is a serious thing going on here, this really isn't the time—"

"Oh, but it is the time. I'm Davie." She looked over to her companion.

"And I'm Dakota."

"And we're volunteers at the Honey Bay shelter, together with Miss Alice. We just wanted to tell you the shelter was badly damaged in the storm yesterday. Miss Alice says fixing it is going to be like a hundred million dollars or something."

I smiled at them. "I think she said a hundred thousand. Not a hundred million."

"Ok, a hundred thousand." Davie shrugged. "Anyway, the shelter doesn't have that kind of money. I don't have that kind of money. I don't think Miss Alice has that kind of money—"

"Oh, girls, I'm sorry." I shook my head preemptively. I was unemployed. I was in no position to donate.

I knew this pitch. Fans came to me with hard-luck stories. More often than not, I just gave them the money instead of going to bed wondering about how they're doing. When Inferno was still active, I might've just written a check for the shelter. But now, as an out-of-work celebrity, I had to be careful about my money.

"What are you apologizing about?" Davie asked.

"I can't help you. I'm sorry. I just quit Inferno." I shook my head firmly. I'd let them down quickly. I was in no position to fund the shelter. "I don't even have a band anymore. I don't have any concerts or albums lined up. I'm basically unemployed. I've got enough money to feed myself for a few months, but I can't donate a hundred thousand dollars. I'm sorry."

"Nooo!" Dakota shook her head. Davie joined her in the head shake. "We're not begging you for money, silly!"

"Oh. Ok." A weight was lifted off of me. I no longer had to feel guilty about turning them down. "Then what?"

"A concert!" The two shouted and nodded in unison. "You could play a benefit concert. To raise money for the animal shelter."

Dakota pointed two fingers at me. "You're a pretty big deal, Mister Dante Huxley."

Davie nodded. "Miss Alice said we could monetize your fame. And that it would be good for your image and could jump-start your career." Davie was carefully repeating all the big words.

"So it's Alice's idea!" I laughed. The two girls looked at each other, embarrassed at having been found out. I shook my head. "Don't worry. It's a very good idea. And I won't tell Miss Alice that I figured out it was her idea. Ok?"

"So you'll play the concert?" Dakota pleaded with her hands in front of her. "Pretty please with sprinkles on top?"

"Um." I couldn't see a reason not to do it. At the same time, I didn't want to risk disappointing two kids. "Did you ever learn at school what a *conditional acceptance* is?"

"No." Davie and Dakota shook their heads in unison, rust-hued curls flying.

"Yeah, you're too young." I sighed. "Alright. I'll do it, as long as it's ok with the town and the shelter. Ok? You guys are the first to know."

The two girls high-fived each other, then high-fived again using opposite hands. "Thanks, Dante Huxley!" they called out in unison. They ran to Alice, who was bantering with Ted again. After Davie and Dakota breathlessly told her something, Alice waved a thumbs-up in my direction.

I walked over to Alice and Ted. "I just agreed to do a benefit concert for the shelter."

"Not a bad idea." Ted nodded. "Solo?"

"Of course solo." I sighed. "I'm over Inferno."

Davie and Dakota appeared again at my sleeve. "Mister Dante!"

"Yeah?"

"We'll need to make posters for the concert, and we'll need you to pose for pictures—" They both covered their faces and giggled into their hands.

"Yeah, I got it. I'll pose for your Instagrams and TikToks and whatever." I smiled and nodded. "I'll pose for the actual concert posters too."

Dakota leaned in and faux-whispered to me: "Miss Alice said you're really nice. She was right."

Ted shook his head at her wistfully. "Ah, the illusions of youth."

Alice clicked her tongue. "Preferable to the rancor of old age." Ted shot her a pretend death stare.

"So, I agreed to do the concert," I said to nobody in particular. "But I don't have any new material."

Alice smiled at Ted. "Well, Ted, you're a songwriter—"

Ted shook like he'd been jolted by a power line. He quickly cleared his throat and pointed at the sky. "Look, all the storm clouds are gone!"

Alice looked embarrassed. That must've been a slip up.

Ted and I walked back to Deep Down and climbed into his Range Rover for the three-minute drive home.

I started to ask Ted: "Hey, since we have some privacy here—"

"Oh, shit, no, I don't wanna get cited for public indecency." Ted laughed.

"Not that, not that. I was just wondering, Ted. Alice mentioned you're a songwriter?"

Ted shook his head. "I think she's going senile." He said it in a way like he had to see a man about a dog.

Of course he didn't really think Alice was going senile. He'd jumped at her words like she'd given him an electrical zap. I wasn't going to pry.

9

Ted

"How's this?" Dante burst into my room at eight P.M., half out of breath from carrying his acoustic guitar upstairs. He stood in front of my bed, cleared his throat, and tuned his guitar strings.

He played a few bars on his guitar and sang a few lines about looking for something and not finding it. After about a quarter of a song, he stood his guitar on the floor. My perfectly polished hardwood floor. And he looked at me like he was expecting applause.

"It's—" I shook my head. It wasn't anything remarkable. I certainly wasn't going to burst out into applause for a quarter of a forgettable, generic pop ditty. "It's not bad, but you holed up in the kitchen supposedly writing songs for two days and all you could come up with is *that*?"

"That's seriously the support you're going to give me?" Dante spun his guitar absentmindedly and looked out the window. "I'm sorry I can't be as brilliant as you, Ted. I would be really happy, though, if you'd be so kind as to give me some minor, basic recognition of my meager musical efforts."

"The truth is never pleasant to hear, Dante." I yawned and lay on my side to try to sleep.

"I just wish you would—" Dante stopped and walked a step closer to my bed. "Are you already asleep?"

I didn't answer. He exhaled loudly and left.

I woke to morning sunlight. Duchess was at my side. Dante wasn't.

He couldn't have moved back into the spare room. The repair people had already closed it off and started work.

He couldn't have been sleeping under my bed. Even his hairstyle wouldn't have fit.

He might've just left.

I showered. Alone. Since he'd started sharing my room, I'd grown accustomed to our grope fests and morning make-out sessions in the shower.

I went downstairs. Dante was still in his same chair at the kitchen table. He was writing in a notebook, hunched over it like he was afraid someone would be cribbing his songs. He wore big studio headphones, plugged in to his laptop. He didn't even see me.

Resting my hand on his shoulder startled him. He took off his headphones, laid down his pen, and looked up at me. "Yeah, Ted? I'm writing. Just my substandard tunes for you to laugh at."

I nodded. "I'm heading off to work." I started to walk toward the door.

My stomach sank. Why was I being such a petulant piece of shit?

I turned right around, back to Dante. "Hey! Can I hear what you've come up with so far?"

"I don't think so." Dante gave me a forced smile. "I don't want to get discouraged by your inevitable wrecking of whatever I've created."

"No, no." I clenched my teeth. I forced myself to say it. "I'm sorry. I'm sorry about what I said last night."

"Alright." Dante smiled up at me. "I'll try again." He took his acoustic guitar in hand. He clicked on his laptop to play the drum intro and backing track.

I stood a few steps back, like a fan in the audience, and started snapping my fingers.

He sang for me. Beautifully. I tapped my foot, snapped my fingers, and clapped for him: everything to show that I appreciated him.

When he finished, he didn't look at me. He clicked on his laptop to stop the backing music. He put down his guitar. His eyes followed it. He muttered: "I know it's not great, but it's what I've got so far." His downcast eyes put me close to tears.

"Dante." I squatted down next to his seat and wrapped my arm around him. "It *is* great. Good lord. You've succeeded in the pop genre how many times already?"

"Only once so far." Dante looked down at the floor, then at me. "Hoping to succeed again solo."

"It's as good as, or better than, your past work. I'm just an idiot, ok? Don't take my bullshit to heart. Your songs are great. I'm serious."

Dante suddenly smiled. "Well that wind turned quickly." He turned the page of his notebook and showed me lines of lyrics scratched out multiple times and rewritten. "I write it all out, lyrics and music, then rewrite and rewrite. Getting closer to good at each pass."

"You don't have Avid Pro Tools?" I asked. I'd known pro music software from my days back in New York — those after-college, eighteen months of mine that Dante didn't know about. "It's great for songwriting. You can change the pitch, mix as you're working, anything you need." Then my face flushed red. "I mean, I've heard Avid Pro Tools is what music professionals use. I've seen ads for it."

"I don't have it." Dante shrugged. "Inferno used to rent a music workstation from the record company. I don't have the software myself."

"Oh. Well. You should consider — I mean so I've heard — you should consider getting Pro Tools for your music."

"Thanks. I'll consider it." Dante smiled. "I've actually got more songs. Can I sing a bit more for you?"

"Yes, please. For your number one fan."

"Don't you have to go to work, mister number one fan?"

"Selling those super-obscure Sigur Ros box sets smuggled in from Iceland can wait." I shrugged and laughed. "Sing it for me again, Dante."

"Alright! Alright!" Dante was all smiles. "Here's another song I wrote, actually. A whole song."

"Go for it!"

"I'll sit back down for this one. This is one of those soulful, mournful singer-songwriter bits." Dante made a soulful, mournful face.

"Kitchen table is all yours." I made the grandiose hand-sweep gesture that Dante always mocked.

Dante sat down and took his guitar in his lap. He grinned at me. "Do I look soulful enough?"

"We need to dim the lights a bit." I hopped over to the kitchen window and shut the blinds, then turned off the overhead kitchen light. "It's, you know, more soulful that way."

"Wow, I feel like Bruno Mars already!" Dante adjusted a nonexistent hat on his head.

"Who?"

"Bruno Mars. He's a—"

"I know who Bruno Mars is." I pretended to adjust an imaginary hat to match Dante's imaginary hat. "I'm just teasing you."

"Well, baby, I'm so soulful." Dante was speaking breathily. "I'm so soulful that I'm gonna sit down at this here kitchen table and sing this here song."

He strummed his guitar and tapped his foot. He sang. I didn't want him to stop. I didn't even want to go to work. I'd been an idiot for disparaging Dante's musical abilities in any form.

He finished the last notes and looked up at me, smiling. I applauded, loudly. "That's soulful as fuck."

"Thanks, I think." Dante laughed.

"I have to go to work now, but your music — it's great. I hope you have another productive day today."

I started opening the blinds again. Dante stopped me. "Keep the blinds closed. I need that soulful mood."

"You don't wanna be naked Florida Man at the window, huh?" I gestured like I was opening my imaginary trench coat.

Dante shrugged. "If I had a dick like yours, I'd stand naked in the window too."

I speed-walked out to my car. Had I not stopped myself, I might've spent all day, and all night, in the kitchen with Dante. Or inside him.

At Deep Down, I went right to my office, and locked the door behind me. Then I went to that locked cabinet behind my desk, the one I usually said had "childhood memories."

Inside: Notebooks, mixtapes, inquiry letters, even the lease to my New York apartment. Not many people knew. Certainly Dante had no idea.

I dug out my old Avid Pro Tools customer ID card. Lifetime discount. I'd spent a few thousand on software, back when I thought I could become a songwriter, those eighteen months "finding myself" in New York City. Almost nobody in Honey Bay knew.

I pulled up the Pro Tools website and got out my credit card. Pro Tools Ultimate. Twenty-six hundred dollars, so be it. Dante needed this for his new career.

When the license code arrived in my email, I printed it out. I even ran to CVS and bought a cheesy card and envelope to put it inside.

What sort of romantic fool was I becoming?

10

Dante

Alice Silver emailed me to confirm the concert was all ready to go. Saturday at eight P.M., I'd be strutting my stuff on stage, all to benefit the Honey Bay Animal Rehabilitation Center. I was too engrossed in my Avid Pro Tools to even see the Gmail notification.

Yes, yes, of course I'd be there. Yes, yes, of course I had material to sing and was ready to interact with the crowd and sign autographs and all that good stuff. According to Alice, people were flying in from as far as Los Angeles to see me play a solo show.

The material to sing was a bit of vaporware. The material didn't exactly... exist. But I'd have it ready before the concert. I had my creative mojo back, at least a little.

Against the backdrop of an orange sunset, Ted's equally orange Range Rover bounced into the driveway. His grin was huge. And genuine. "Turned the music world upside down yet, solo superstar?" He set an iced coffee on the desk next to me.

"Trying to." I pointed at my laptop screen. "Pro Tools helped a lot. Thank you for that. Your emotional support helped even more though. Thank you for that too."

Ted glanced down at the laptop screen full of chord progressions, then stopped himself. "I don't even know what I'm looking at." He laughed nervously. "I'm glad I bought you the right thing. With as much as I know about music software, I might've bought you Leisure Suit Larry."

"Vintage!" I looked up at Ted and laughed. "And speaking of vintage, I'm still using pen-and-paper as well." I opened the notebook and showed him my pages of scribbles.

"How many tracks in are you?" Ted clicked his tongue. He sounded like an industry pro. I'd never heard a mere fan talking like that. Maybe it was just from his owning a music store.

"Four and a half done. I'm hoping to do seven completely new songs for the benefit concert. I mean, they're kind of rough still, but completely new, original music and lyrics and what have you."

"That's an impressive pace." Ted squeezed and drummed on my shoulders, like a mini-massage.

"Right now I'm trying to figure out the ending for the fifth song."

"What's it about?" Ted snapped his fingers in the air and swayed his head like a fangirl.

"Cheery, silly love song. Old married couple. Over-the-top, tongue-in cheek sugary. Ed Sheeran meets Otis Redding meets Weird Al." I sang the first few lines.

"That's ridiculous and also very good." Ted nodded.

"Thanks. But I'm still only four-and-a-half songs done on a seven-song set. That doesn't even include practice."

"Four and a half out of seven, so you're about sixty-five percent done." Ted smiled and clapped my back to signal the end of the five-minute massage. "And it took you what, two weeks to get that far? That's impressive."

"Yeah. I needed my laptop calculator to do that math. Only sixty-five percent. But I'm still going pretty fast." I sighed. "The normal musician timeline for writing five new songs is what, like a year?"

"Unless you're Brian Wilson." Ted laughed. "Then it's forty years."

"The *Smile* album?" I gave Ted a thumbs-up. "Oh yeah, you *would* know that."

"I know a thing or two about music. Just as an outside fan." Ted shrugged and laughed. "I'm gonna go upstairs, feed Duchess, and rest for a while. Work well. Shout if you need anything."

"I already split a turkey sandwich with Duchess, but she told me not to tell you." I put my finger to my lips. "And yeah, thanks. I also might need a break soon."

Ted squatted next to my chair and hugged me. He got up and started up the stairs. "Do great. I won't bother you."

"I think that hug is exactly what I needed."

I went back to the song, first on the laptop, then on pen and paper. I stood up and walked around the living room and looked out the window. Tapped on the window. Opened it and closed it.

Then back to the kitchen table. Still no new lyrics.

I took a deep breath, closed my notebook, and shut down the laptop. I'd go get some distraction upstairs.

Quietly, I opened Ted's door. He lay on top of his comforter, naked, with eyes closed. His legs were propped up like he was about to raise his ass, but his ass wasn't going anywhere.

His cock stood up, completely erect. And his hand was on it. He stroked and pumped his dick slowly, but deliberately enough that he was definitely awake.

I knelt next to the bed and stared close-up at Ted masturbating. It was fucking hot: his hand grope-squeezing his foreskin and shaft, his fingers occasionally running over his moistened cocktip.

This was how Ted jacked off. This was definitely how he liked his dick fondled.

I blew air at his dick. Startled, Ted opened his eyes. "I thought it was an approaching cold front."

"It's just an exhausted songwriter." I sighed.

"Me or you?"

"Me. I was just sitting in the kitchen writing songs."

"Oh. Yeah." Ted seemed strangely relieved. "Well, there are always recreational and athletic activities available in this bed."

"Are you inviting me to hide the salami?" I burst out laughing.

"That's an Andy Silver level joke." Ted rolled his eyes. "I'd prefer to invite you to an evening of making the beast with two backs." He was still slowly stroking his dick. Precum dripped from the tip onto his hand.

"Ooh, the beast with two backs!" I gave Ted a double thumbs-up. I crawled into bed on all fours, stared down at his hand wrapped around his hard dick.

I kissed the base of his cock and licked in a circle where his shaft met his ballsack. Then I sucked on the entire ballsack to take it all in my mouth. I loudly slurped on it while looking in Ted's eyes.

I licked the tip of his dick, just above his hand. "Ted, I think you can go hands-free now."

He laughed and moved his hand away from his dick. He ran his hand through my hair.

I stared into his trimmed pubic hair. I lowered my mouth down onto his fat dick. I opened my lips enough to take his girth inside me. He was super hard.

I savored the sweet saltiness of his precum and I ran my tongue over the veins along his shaft. I pushed my head down more, until his dick was at my throat. I'd never thought the sight, feeling, and taste of a dick would make me horny. Now, I couldn't imagine anything more erotic than Ted's dick stuffed in my mouth.

I bobbed my head up and down and groped at his balls. I squeezed and fondled them in my fingers. With my other hand, I teased at Ted's ass.

He raised his ass, doing the yoga-like position again. I licked one of my fingers to make it slippery, then slipped that finger inside him. He moaned.

My finger explored the warm tightness inside Ted's butthole. He gasped when I managed to tickle his prostate.

I pulled my finger out halfway, then pushed it all the way in. Ted bit his lip and sighed. I pulled out and in and got a rhythm going, finger-fucking his ass.

He moved his hand down to his hard dick again. I kissed his hand and licked through the spaces between his fingers to lick his dick.

I gave his hand a little love bite. "Let me ride your dick. I want you inside me."

"Mmm." Ted nodded so enthusiastically he looked like he'd hurt his neck. "I'm ready for you."

"What about my dry ass?" I laughed. "Put on a condom and I'll lube up."

I reached over to the nightstand for the bottle of lube. Ted reached into the drawer of that same nightstand for a condom. He'd started keeping a whole box of condoms there, instead of the solitary condom in his wallet just hoping for a chance at deployment.

Ted and I were getting a familiarity in our sex. We could joke. We knew each other's bodies. Maybe I'd never even gotten to that point with any woman — but I'd never been enthusiastic about sex with any woman. I'd had sex with women, mostly Kate, only because it was expected of a pop star.

Ted tossed the condom wrapper into the trash and showed off his latex-wrapped dick. "I've donned my chapeau, monsieur!"

"Well then." I lay on my stomach and reached back to pour some lube in my ass. Then I put more lube on my hand and coated my rim with it. "We're off to the races, I guess."

"Mixed metaphor." Ted sighed, still jerking his dick.

I straddled his crotch and leaned down to kiss him, lips to lips, tongue on tongue.

Ted grabbed at my ass cheeks and tickled inside my rim. "I can finger your ass too, you know." He slid his fingers inside.

"I'm well aware of that." I laughed and slowly lowered that same ass off of Ted's fingers and onto the tip of Ted's dick.

Ted shrugged as best he could lying down. "Well, why use my fingers for what I can do with my dick!" He held his cock in position while I leaned forward, straddling him. I balanced my body just right so I could kiss his forehead — but it was a precarious pose, on the verge of falling onto him.

"Hey." Ted looked up at me with a smile through his gray eyes. "This is sex, not an acrobatic exhibition."

"Oh yeah. Just plain old anal sex. Nothing to see here." I lowered myself completely down onto his condomed dick.

It didn't even have that intense stretching-out feeling that it had given me the first time around. It just felt like Ted was filling me up with all of himself. Anal sex was the usual for me now. If it felt at all unusual, it was only unusual in the most thrilling way: a route to sexual pleasure I'd never before taken. Before meeting Ted, I hadn't even thought about it.

Ted thrust up into me. His dick hit that same spot on my prostate that his fingers had tickled.

The mirror on his bedroom closet looked like a projection of porn. I'd never imagined myself starring in gay porn, and loving it.

I held on to Ted's sides, like holding on to a saddle. He pushed up fucking me harder and faster. I started playing with my dick, the same leisurely way he'd been playing with his dick when I'd walked in on him.

Every time Ted thrust into me, it was a big deal. He groaned. The force of him pushing into me rocked me forward. The bed squeaked. And every time, I responded with a leisurely push and pull on my dick.

I didn't want to overstimulate. Staring at Ted's face, his chest, his hard nipples, his meaty belly, I was always on the verge of shooting my load all over him. He was stimulating enough.

Ted was thrusting up into my ass in a steady rhythm, his eyes half-closed. He opened his eyes and looked at me. "So how's songwriting going?"

"Needing a few more lines of lyrics."

"For the silly song?" Ted slapped my ass as I rode back and forth on his dick.

"Yeah, for the silly song." I leaned forward a bit to kiss Ted. He beat me to it: he sat up, while still fucking my ass, and planted a wet kiss on my lips. "You know, romance, love, silly stuff like that." I grinned at Ted.

He grabbed my thighs and closed his eyes as he kept fucking me, harder and harder. His pubes hit my ass every time and his dick was planting itself deep enough to touch my prostate.

He gently pulled my hand off my cock. He sucked on my fingers while looking into my eyes. He pointed my dick at his face and smiled, then jerked me in rhythm to his power-fucking of my ass from below.

"Oh fuck, Ted." It was that tingling in my dick and balls again. It went all over my body, even up to my nipples.

"Problem?" Ted was laughing as he fucked me and stroked my dick.

"Oh fuck. I'm gonna—" I closed my eyes and groaned. My hips thrust forward. My dick crashed into Ted's hand. I shot my cum onto Ted's chest and face.

He smiled and opened his mouth in time for my second rope of cum: again on his chest, with just enough in his mouth. He licked it off his lips.

Ted's thrusting grew frantic, like a jackhammer. He was pulling me down at the hips so his dick could go deeper in me. He leaned up and kissed me. His whole face was sweaty. My ass felt like a freshly mashed potato.

His legs and hips shook under me. He thrust up so hard he almost threw me off. He breathed faster and faster. His dick throbbed and pumped. Even his balls right below me were throbbing and pumping. His condom deep inside me filled with hot cum.

"Did you just make a cummy?" I smiled down at him. I was still rocking back and forth atop his dick, like his crotch was a pony ride.

"Like, several cummies." He smiled while wiping sweat from his face.

I gyrated one last full circle with his dick still in me. "Just making sure we've got every last drop in that condom."

"Oh yeah." Ted shook his head. "We're not even at the fuel low light. My balls are way-down-to-zero empty."

"I have no problems emptying your balls." I pulled my ass up slowly off his dick. I reached under my crotch and slipped off his condom, tied it at the top, and three-pointed it into the trash can. It all felt so familiar and natural now. Sex with Kate had never been so easy. "Nor do I have any problems disposing of your chapeau."

"You don't have any problems doing anything you put your mind or your ass to." Ted wrapped his arms behind my back and brought me down to lie on top of him. He kissed my neck, then my lips. "Mmm, your mouth tastes like coffee."

"Coffee and trying to finish the last song. Story of my life." I sighed.

"The silly love song?" Ted punctuated his question with a wet kiss on my lips. "Tell me how it goes."

I sighed and rolled off of Ted to lie on my side. I pressed my head into his shoulder, the same way I always slept with him. "It's stupid though."

Ted whispered: "Stupid songs are the ones that make money." He laughed. "So tell me."

"Well." I sighed. "Ok, it's stupid, but it's this elderly couple, and the husband is singing all these cheesy lyrics to his wife — or maybe his husband — saying like being in love with you is even better than gardening."

"Alright." Ted nodded. "I'm feeling it. So tell me about the part that's got you stuck?"

"So he's saying, *Love caught us, Cupid's arrow.*" I looked up at Ted, expecting him to wince or grumble at the cheesiness. He didn't. "I know it's cheesy, ok? But I need a few more lines to finish it up."

"Sing it for me." Ted gave my forehead a small, encouraging kiss. "Just the last line will do."

I sang for him. "Love caught us, Cupid's arrow." I felt self-conscious, but at least he was no longer ridiculing my music.

"*Alright, alright.*" Ted inhaled deeply and propped his head up on the pillow. "How about this? *This love is no wheelbarrow, You're sweet like a marshmallow, Our field of daisies will never run fallow.*"

"Oh my God." I broke out laughing. "That's amazing."

"And then you can finish it up." Ted held one finger in the air. "*Hello, key lime yellow, play the cello.*"

I laughed hard enough to curl up into the fetal position laughing. "Ted." I looked at him, shaking my head. "It's so bad that it's good. I swear. I love it."

"It's just something off the top of my head." Ted shrugged.

I tapped Ted's lyrics into my phone notepad so I wouldn't forget them. "Ted. You've got obvious talent. And you know music. You should try to get into songwriting. Like, professionally."

"Did Duchess have her dinner yet?" Ted peered out the bedroom door.

"Twice already today." I shrugged. "But who's counting?"

"Thanks." Ted smiled. "I'm going to sleep now." Ted moved the pillow so his head occupied only half of it. "Feel free to join me whenever work allows."

"I'll work for a few more hours, I think. Your lines inspired me to go on to the next songs."

"Glad to help. An outsider sometimes gives you a change of scenery, a new perspective, you know?" He lay on his side, his perfectly meaty ass peeking out from under the comforter.

"Yeah." I smiled at Ted and his perfect ass.

"Hey, are you viewing my gluteal scenery?"

"Maybe." I grinned. He knew me well. I couldn't stop staring at his ass, clothed or otherwise. "Tomorrow, can I tag along with you to Deep Down? No offense to the kitchen table, but it gets a little boring."

"Sure." Ted shrugged. "Mi casa, tu casa. Mi assa, tu assa." Drowsily, he slapped his ass cheek and closed his eyes to sleep.

Downstairs, I transcribed Ted's suggestion into my fifth song. My next two songs were waiting for me, but resting in Ted's arms was that much more appealing.

I closed my laptop and went upstairs to bed.

Ted woke me with soft kisses on my neck while the morning sun blazed outside and Duchess meowed for her breakfast. I stayed in bed and told him I'd walk over to Deep Down a bit later.

After I dragged myself out of bed and showered, the walk to Deep Down Music already felt like an everyday routine. I carried my laptop — Pro Tools installed on it — in a shoulder bag, and plopped down with it in the store's listening lounge.

I waved at Ted. He was busy with a customer, but smiled and waved back to me.

Angelica took notice of me. She almost ran over to where I was sitting. Then she stopped and started studiously, laboriously dusting a rack of vinyl records. With each sweep of her duster, she looked over at me, with a smile.

It was that "hey, will you please say something to me so I can start talking to you?" smile people gave celebrities. Or at least gave me.

Angelica was always a stable presence in Ted's store: Ted had his moods, but Angelica always greeted me with her friendly smile. And she was obviously a hard worker. She was dusting and polishing those vinyl records like they were about to go into a cleanroom. I nodded to acknowledge her efforts. "Those are going to be the cleanest LPs the world has ever seen."

"Ted has his standards." She smiled at me, then very obviously looked me up and down. She was probably referring to more than his vinyl record cleanliness standards.

"Ted is a really talented guy. And not just running the store. Yesterday he helped me write some song lyrics."

"Oh yeah?" Angelica laughed. "He let that out?"

"The lyrics? Yeah, he wrote some lines for me. Just off the top of his head. It was amazing. He's like a professional songwriter."

"He *is* a professional songwriter." Angelica rolled her eyes, then glanced at where Ted was lecturing a customer over a CD boxed set. "Or he was, at least."

"Really? Ted?" That explained a lot. "He can write songs?"

"He has a degree in songwriting. He spent time trying to make it big in New York. Something like that."

"Really?" My eyes were wide open. "He never told me about that." I laid my laptop on the sofa and went over to Ted. He stood behind the cash register, arms folded, staring out the window.

"Hey, Ted!" I stood directly in front of him. "Angelica says you're a professional songwriter! I still need two more songs, so—"

"I'm a what?" He scowled at me, like I'd just insulted him.

"You're a professional songwriter. I can definitely use some help. I wonder if you could—" I felt like I was trying to talk to a celebrity.

"Get out of here, Dante." Ted shook his head. I'd never heard his voice so gruff, not even the first day he'd met me on his lawn. "This is a place of business, not your personal relaxation lounge. You're disturbing the customers."

"What?" I half-smiled. Maybe he was joking and I'd missed the setup, and the punchline.

"Really, just get out of here, Dante. You're loitering in my store." Still scowling, he shook his head at me.

"Ah." I looked at him. He still didn't seem like he was joking. "Ok." I walked out. I looked back one last time. He wasn't laughing or chasing after me. There hadn't been a joke I'd missed.

I walked back home. At the kitchen table, I tried to write, but I felt like shit.

11

Ted

"Ted." Angelica came at me full force with her schoolmarmish speedwalk. She had that face, that look, and that walk: she was going to talk down to me right in my own store. "Ted, you can't—" She was shaking her head the way she always did.

"I can't what?" I buried my head in the point-of-sale screen, pretending to be entirely engrossed in the listing of the three transactions we'd had that day. "This is my store. This is my life. Whatever I want, I can."

"Fine, you *can*." Angelica pulled up a retail-bitch stool just like mine and sat right next to me. I shrunk from her a bit. She had that look like she was going to put her arm around me: an eventuality I'd spent my whole life avoiding. "Ted, you *can* alienate everyone who cares about you. There's no law against it. But you're not going to be happy with the results."

"Can you please at least explain what alleged behavior of mine you're referring to?" I gave her a look meant to scare her away, but this time, just like every time, it only seemed to encourage her.

"You know." She sighed.

"No, I don't know." I put my hands in the air: the ultimate gesture of frustration. "If I'm going to be drawn and quartered, I'd at least like to know for what offense."

"Ted." There went Angelica's arm. That gentle pat on my back. "You've been doing this ever since—"

"Ok, fine." I interrupted what was about to become a thorough shaming of my lack of interpersonal skills and devotion to certain standards of behavior. "You don't need to recount the full laundry list of gory details."

"So? Are you hearing me here?"

"I'm hearing you, Angelica." I stood up and looked around the store. At least whatever barbs anyone threw my way, Deep Down Music was always mine, free and clear, and in my own store, I was king. "I'm hearing you, but are you pulling me over the coals because I told Dante not to loiter in my store? I've seen you kick loiterers out of my store. Why can't I?"

"You can, you can, *you can*!" She shook her head like I was stupid. Maybe I was, a little. "You *can* do anything, Ted. But you'll end up lonely and bitter, and friendships and love will have passed you by."

"So dramatic." I shook my head. "I tell a loitering guy I've known for only a month to get out of my store, and suddenly I'm going to end up an angry old spinster?"

"Ted." She shook her head again, that very same infuriating way. "Dante seems to really like you. And be able to put up with you. It's like you resent him for putting up with you. Like you're going to punish him for that."

"Are you saying I'm difficult to put up with?" I looked at her. She didn't say anything. "Ok, maybe I am."

"I swear, Ted." She was whispering now. This was definitely going to be some heavy shit. She never whispered except for really heavy shit. "Ted, even I sometimes have to take some alone time away from you. I've known you since kindergarten, ok, I know you're a good guy despite your outbursts — but someone who doesn't know you that well? They'll just walk away from you. Or run."

"So what you're saying is" — I cleared my throat — "is that I'm such a sorry-ass, friendless loser that I'd better be grateful that anybody even speaks to me, much less wants to date me. And I should be so grateful as to let him walk over me. Is that right?"

She cracked her knuckles in frustration. "What you and I say here in your music store doesn't matter, Ted. No matter what defense you come up with right now, what clever comebacks you throw at me. You're still pushing away people who care about you. That's what matters at the end of the day. You can't change that with a clever comeback, Ted."

"I'm going to—" I glanced at my stuffy back-room office. No, hiding out there would've been too much like handing victory to Angelica: conceding the store to her, hiding myself in shame in the scullery. No. I'd exercise my full power as boss. "Angelica, I'm going to take the rest of the day off. Personal day. Bye."

Just like that. My store. My life. My day off. I stepped out of that place and walked down the street. I was the owner. I could even park in the Deep Down parking lot when I wasn't shopping there. Let Angelica, Dante, whoever else think they could fuck with me — at least I still entirely controlled some things. My days off and my parking spot, among them.

At least the weather wasn't fucking with me. The storm was long gone. The day was warm without the blazing heat of truly hot days, and the sun was warm, but not blinding.

Rawlins Telecom wasn't the greatest cellphone carrier, but they'd done an admirable job sprucing up the WHON building. It looked respectable without losing its community radio feel.

I stopped for a few seconds to admire the building from across the street. I'd rarely had the chance to just walk by it, rather than driving.

Andy Silver stepped out of the station. "Ted Baker! Shouldn't you be at your store, complaining about today's pop music?"

I sighed. "I'm apparently PNG, persona non grata, over there."

"At your own store?" Andy took a step back and looked at me. Of course he knew there was more to the story. He pointed ahead on the sidewalk. "I'm going to walk around the block while we play half an hour of music. Join me if you'd like."

"So." I cleared my throat. Andy usually understood my troubles. "I politely asked a loitering non-customer to vacate the premises. In my own store, mind you. Angelica immediately got all up in my face about it, saying I'll end up sad and alone if I keep being like that."

"Hmm." Andy sucked his lips into his mouth. "Let me guess: the loitering customer was not just some random dude?"

I clasped my hands behind my back, like I was hiding a magic trick. "It depends." I nodded at him seriously. "On exactly what *not just some random dude* is."

"Alright." Andy sighed. "Did you get into a spat with Dante?"

"Yes." I felt like a schoolboy confessing in the principal's office. "He was pushing the songwriter thing in my face."

Andy walked a half-step ahead of me so he could keep turning his head and staring creepily straight into my eyes. "You mean he brought up the Big Forbidden Topic? That he'd somehow gotten wind of?"

"You know?" I clenched my teeth as I asked him. I'd assumed only Angelica knew.

"Ted. Let me tell you a little on-secret." Andy shook his head. "Everyone pretends they don't know that you went to New York for two years after college trying to break into songwriting and came back with your tail between your quite muscular and toned legs, I must say." I was wearing shorts and Andy was looking down and appreciating the view.

"Thanks. I do leg presses." I shrugged. "Anyway, everybody knows? How?"

"Uh, NYU has a picture of you on its songwriting program alumni page?" Andy laughed. "Google easily links your name to lots of unsold songs listed for sale online? Your stuff is still on Soundcloud and Bandcamp?"

"You didn't mention: it's also still on MySpace." I shook my head.

"Well, I didn't want to be cruel." Andy laughed. "So Dante was asking you about songwriting or something? And you kicked him out?"

"I just didn't want somebody digging through my life history like that. Knowing me like that. I keep some things to myself."

"Alright, Ted." Andy stopped walking and laid his hand on my arm. "Let's think now. You're a music store owner. Your friend, special friend, whatever, is a music star. You're helping him write songs. Don't you think it's reasonable that the secret would somehow come out that you're trained as a professional songwriter?"

"Maybe." I looked down, then started walking again. "Maybe I'm just too used to living completely solo. On my terms."

"The way I see it." Andy lowered his voice, like he was going to tell me a secret. "You let Angelica close to you because she's your employee and depends on you for her livelihood. Just like back in high school, she depended on you to do her calculus homework."

"How did you know about that?" I stared at him and shook my head.

"She asked me to fill in once when you were at home sick. I was a freshman. I laughed at her and said sorry, I'm gay, I don't do homework for pretty girls."

"Andy. You didn't know I was a big flaming trombone-playing homo?" I was laughing so hard I stopped mid-step to catch my breath.

"You were a senior. I thought you were a straight, popular band guy, that Angelica was your girlfriend, and that I was the only gay guy in the whole school." Andy smiled and shrugged. "Anyway, as I was saying." He cleared his throat, somewhat officiously.

"Yes, as you were saying, Andy."

"Angelica is safe for you because you've known her for a long time, she knows the boundaries with you, and she's still not as close as a spouse or boyfriend would be." Andy snapped his tongue for emphasis. Maybe he was waiting for me to object to his observations. There was nothing to object to. "And Duchess, you're ok with Duchess because she depends on you for food and she doesn't know how to talk, alright?"

"Cold but true." I nodded. "You do know your stuff."

"I don't know if you've been listening to *Andy in the A.M.*"

"Not as often as I should. I'm usually still asleep, then at work."

"Well, it's become more of an advice show in the past couple of years. Settling down, getting married to Baxter, living in that McMansion you loathe — it made me Uncle Andy who can give advice."

"You're, what..." I counted idly on my fingers. "You're four years younger than me. But your life is so together, you know?"

"Nah." Andy's smile sort of betrayed that he was thinking Yah even when he was saying Nah. "I just married my high school sweetheart and have my dream job at a radio station."

"Well, I didn't have a high school sweetheart." I shrugged. "And of course being a songwriter was my dream. Of course. But running a music store isn't so bad."

"What if you could break out of that, dude?" Andy suddenly did a tap dance on the sidewalk, as much as his half-untied Chucks allowed.

"And go into professional tap dancing?"

"You've got the legs for it." Andy coughed. "I didn't just say that. But no, I mean, try for what you really really want, instead of sticking to what's just sort of good enough."

"Yeah, where's my break into the songwriting world?" I sighed.

Andy stared at me like I was missing something obvious. "Are you forgetting?"

"Oh. Yeah. Dante." I slapped my forehead for comedic effect. "Dante asked me to help him write some songs. That's why I chased him out of my store."

"So that made you uncomfortable." Andy nodded like an experienced psychotherapist. "Because it was simultaneously two possibilities of going from *ok* to *what you really want*. Dante presumably is offering you a relationship. A love relationship, not just a hookup with whatever college scuba diving club is in town."

"How do you know about that?" My jaw dropped a little.

"I saw the scuba tanks outside your door every night for a week?" Andy laughed.

"Subletters. Those belonged to subletters." I nodded. Innocently.

"Whatever." Andy shook his head like he didn't believe me. "Dante is offering you a real, long-term relationship. And a career as a songwriter. Or at least a gig as a songwriter. And those possibilities are so perfect that you're scared of them."

"Yikes." I nodded. Like always, Andy had spoken the truth. "The truth hurts, Andy. The truth hurts."

"Welcome to real life, I guess?" Andy pointed at WHON across the street. "Speaking of which, I have to get back to real life. My job. Nice walking and chatting with you though."

"Like always. You gave me food for thought." I squeezed Andy's arm goodbye. "Thank you again. I'll let you know how it goes."

I trudged back in the direction of Deep Down to get my car. The early afternoon sun was in full bloom, but still not so bad. At least living in Honey Bay was one thing in my life that was already perfect, not just good enough or second best.

I stood on the corner waiting for the crossing light. A black car with Uber stickers blew by me so quickly I could feel the wind. The passenger had Dante's facial profile, Dante's hairstyle — maybe it was Dante. Maybe he'd finally up and left.

The thought of that hurt, as much as I didn't want to admit it to myself. Everything around my store now reminded me of Dante. Even the stupid listening lounge inside where I'd told him to scram. Even my car parked outside — the car we always took grocery shopping and cruising around.

I climbed up into the ancient Range Rover and turned on the engine. My phone rang. Dante.

"Hello." I tried to be informal, noncommittal — whether he was calling to apologize or chew me out, I'd go along with it.

"It's all my fault, Ted." Dante spoke quickly. "I'm really, really sorry. I can't apologize enough." Something was beeping in the background wherever he was, maybe a supermarket checkout aisle.

"Oh, don't worry. It's just a little argumen—"

"No. Ted. I left the gate open."

"I told you not to do that."

"Ted. A car hit Duchess."

"A— what—"

"I'm at Doctor Bryson's clinic."

"I'll be there." Emergency blinkers flashing, I went right through one red light, then another. Fuck the tickets. I'd pay them. I arrived at the clinic in what must've been one minute flat.

Dante stood at the clinic's reception counter. I walked past him. I didn't need to acknowledge his presence. Or even his existence.

"I'm Ted Baker," I walked toward the back area and shouted to the first assistant I spotted. "I'm here for my cat, Duchess, hit by a car."

"Hold on, sir." The assistant waved me back out to the waiting area. "The vet will be out to talk with you."

"I need to know—" I controlled myself, not to yell, not to make a scene. What good was it anyway? Even if I didn't make a scene? Duchess was still hit by a car. No matter how much I took anybody's good advice, the end result was still beyond terrible.

"Hold on, sir." The assistant held his hand in front of his face again, like a mime pushing a wall.

"I'm Doctor Linda Bryson." The short, stout woman wore a stethoscope. I did my best to read the news from her expression. Maybe the news wouldn't be all bad, because she didn't look like she had bad news to deliver.

"Nice to meet you." I shook her hand more perfunctorily than I'd shaken anybody's hand in my life. "But how's Duchess?"

"She'll be fine." Doctor Bryson smiled. "She'll need to stay here a couple of days, but she'll be fine, good as new."

Tears rolled down my face. "What happened to her?"

"Well, you already know, probably. Car. Blunt force trauma. She's got some minor fractures, just banged up a little bit. Nothing that cats aren't used to. It wasn't too bad."

"Thank you." I wiped tears from my face. "Can I see her? Is she in pain?"

"Yes and maybe." The doctor nodded and took me back to a room where Duchess lay sleeping, with tubes connected to her mouth and more lines going to her neck. "We're giving her IV painkillers, but honestly, I can't guarantee that she's feeling super chipper right now. The morphine should take effect in about thirty minutes. If she could talk, I could do a better job of telling you what she's feeling."

"Yeah." I stared off at the wall. "Communication is key."

"Huh?" The doctor looked at me.

"Just some life advice." I sighed, staring at Duchess. "So she'll be here in the hospital tonight?"

"Yup. She'll have surgery first thing tomorrow morning. We're going to put some fasteners where her bones broke." The doctor tapped on a laptop and showed me x-ray images of fractures. "Give her a week to recover here. When she gets home, have her more sitting around and less running around."

"The first time Duchess has heard that advice." I laughed and softly petted her belly.

"Yeah." Doctor Bryson shrugged. "We can work on her weight once she's healed from the accident. Give it a couple of months and she'll be active again."

"Thank you." I leaned down to Duchess and kissed her head while she slept. "Thank you."

Doctor Bryson softly pulled me away from Duchess. "Should we keep in touch with you or your — I'm sorry, friend, partner? — the gentleman who brought her in?" The vet pointed at Dante sitting in the waiting room like an idiot, his hoodie popped up.

"Not him." That came out even angrier than I'd intended. "I will be your contact. Don't contact him." I took out my wallet, my business cards inside it. I gave one card to the vet and another to her assistant.

"Oh, Ted Baker, Deep Down, you're the music store guy!" Doctor Bryson smiled and nodded. "People are scared to go to your store because you're so passionate about stuff." She laughed.

"Passionate about a lot of things." I sighed and looked back at Duchess. I handed my Visa card to the assistant. "You can just put the charges on there."

"Oh, we already charged that gentleman's credit card." The assistant pointed back at Dante again. "He said to make sure to bill him and not you."

"Whatever." I shook my head. "Thank you. Give me a call, email, text, anytime with updates on my cat. I think you can tell how much Duchess means to me."

"Absolutely." The vet held my hand in both her hands and nodded me goodbye. She returned to the back room. I came back out to the waiting room, where Dante was sitting.

I shook my head at Dante. "You don't need to be here."

12

Dante

Ted was hurting. Obviously. So was I. So was Duchess.

I tried not to be wounded by Ted's words. I apologized again. And again. "I'm extremely sorry. It was all my fault." My voice shook more every time I said it.

"What was your fault?" Ted was almost yelling at me, like he was challenging me to confess what I'd done. Someone from inside the veterinarian's office peeked out at us. We must've been making a scene.

"I know I left the gate open. I'm sorry. It won't happen again." I stared at the floor tiles between us. Tears dripped down my face.

"It won't happen *again*?" Ted shook his head like I just wasn't understanding. Like I'd insulted him by even trying to apologize. "You're not coming back to my house. Find a new place to stay. Immediately. You're evicted. I'll UPS your belongings to your new address."

I took a step back. With a few words, Ted had just taken away the new life I'd started. It was like he'd pulled out the rug from everything I'd thought I'd found, everything that was going to be my new happiness. If Ted was just having a moment, his moment was lasting quite a while.

The veterinarian's assistant walked out and looked at the two of us with visible discomfort. Ted was causing public drama, but he had the right, maybe. I'd just done something worse than stupid. His cat, his baby, was hurt, and easily could've been killed.

"I'm sorry—" I said the only thing I could think of. What other words were there?

"I'm the one who's sorry." Ted stared at me. He must've been waiting for my reaction. "Sorry to myself, to the life I've built, even to my cat." Ted's face was bright red. He pointed a finger at me. "Because I've lowered myself to consort with some boy band bimbo who showed up at my door."

"I know you're angry, Ted." I breathed deeply. Ted's words hurt me, even if I tried to steel myself against them.

"I shouldn't have even rented to you. Boy band pop star upstyle hairdo." Ted sneered at me. Actually sneered. No one had sneered at me before. "Even for renting the apartment, I have standards."

"I know you're feeling pain, Ted. In whatever way I can help you—" I held my arm out. He ignored it.

"You're not going to be helping me. I'm not going to let you quote unquote help me."

"Anything I can do, Ted. I'm sorry."

"You can not come back to my house is what you can do. I don't need you, Duchess doesn't need you, and I can do just fine without your money."

"I—" I was actually crying. "I'll wait for your call if you ever change your mind." I stepped outside.

I didn't want to be in Ted's field of vision back in the waiting room. Even if I deserved Ted's wrath, he didn't deserve to see any more of my sorry self. Leaving was the only way not to aggravate the situation.

I stood outside the vet clinic. Afternoon school buses passed by as if nothing was wrong. As if the rug hadn't just been pulled out from under my life. I took out my phone and ordered an Uber to the Honey Bay Inn.

My eyes watered in the sun's glare. I was crying too. After a few minutes outside, my face already felt burnt.

The car pulled up. I got in.

"For Dante?" The driver stared at me with that gaze of celebrity-recognition. I wasn't crying, not at that moment anyway. "Aren't you — aren't you Dante Huxley?"

"Yup." I sighed. I didn't have the energy to make up a story about being a Dante Huxley lookalike in town to play a wedding.

"Staying at the Honey Bay Inn?"

"Yup."

"People around town say you were renting an apartment in somebody's house."

"Yeah. It was — it was damaged by the storm. So I have to move out."

"Oh, that sucks." The driver took out a pen and his cardboard Uber placard and handed them both to me in the back seat. "Hey, would you mind—"

"Yeah, I can sign." No matter how shitty I felt, I couldn't let the fans down. I signed. With a flourish. And a smiley face. It was always the smiley face.

"Thanks, man." The driver nodded. "This will go for at least a hundred bucks on Ebay."

I winced a little. But I wasn't going to stop him from cashing in on his famous passenger. Even if it made me feel like a prize steer. I nodded my approval.

He dropped me off at the Honey Bay Inn.

A grandmotherly woman read a gardening magazine behind the check-in counter. Maybe it was a gift from the universe and she wouldn't make me hand over ID and a credit card. Or if she did, maybe at least she wasn't up on her boy-band stars and there would be no awkward conversation about where I was going and where I had been.

"I need a room. Just for tonight. Can I pay cash?"

"You don't have a credit card?" Her expression turned from sweet-grandmother-serving-cookies to neighborhood-watch attack-granny.

My wanting to pay with cash must've triggered just about all of her alarms. Good thing I didn't have a tattoo.

"I do. I just want to pay with cash."

"That doesn't sound right to me." She shook her head.

"Alright." I relented. I pulled down my hoodie, showed her my New York driver's license in the name of *Dante Huxley*, and handed over the credit card with that same name.

Dante Huxley was the last person I wanted to be.

And Dante Huxley was the last person anybody I cared about wanted to be with: first Kate, and now Ted. Maybe my supposed fans would soon dump me too.

Maybe this woman was one of my former fans who'd already dumped me.

"Oh! Dante Huxley!" She wasn't exclaiming. She was squealing. "Dante Huxley, staying at our hotel! I heard you're here in Honey Bay!"

"Yeah." I nodded.

"Your eyes look bloodshot." She gave me an investigative once-over. Maybe she thought I was a drug fiend.

"I've been crying. That's why I've got to stay in a hotel tonight. Ok?" Laying it all out for her immediately might've been less painful than Chinese water torture of a million questions.

"Oh! I heard about you and Kate!" The clerk covered her mouth. "What a sad story!"

"Yeah. So, can I have a room, please? I just need to get to sleep."

"Oh, yes, certainly, Mister Huxley!" She was in kowtow-to-celebrity mode now. Whatever. I just needed a pillow to cry into.

She handed me the key card. She had a final look at my driver's license photo, and smiled at it, before returning my license and credit card.

The elevator brought me upstairs. The key card opened the door. My own legs carried me to the bed.

Ted was just my landlord, I kept trying to convince myself. *Ted was just some random guy in a small town in Florida. I could download a gay dating app and find another man to come out of the closet with.*

None of it worked. None of it sounded convincing in my inner monologue. None of it made me feel any better. I didn't believe any of my clumsily constructed lies to myself.

I'd never felt like this about losing Kate. I didn't really feel anything about losing Kate. I just hated the insult of having been lied to and publicly made a fool of. If she'd just honestly broken up with me, I would've forgotten all about the whole mistake.

I lay face up, contemplating loneliness, Ted, and how I'd fucked up everything.

13

Ted

I hadn't expected to feel so crushingly lonely in the empty house. Duchess was at the vet. Dante was out of my life. I could take it.

But not very well.

I actually opened a can of cat food. I set it in the usual place for Duchess. Not doing it would've felt even worse than doing it.

What was next — talking to an imaginary Dante at the kitchen table? I sighed at my own ridiculousness. I tossed the cat food down the disposal. My heart felt like it had already spent time in its grinding blades.

I spent the night with my own thoughts. Angelica was right. I invariably chased away anyone who dared to care about me. I hadn't even spoken to my parents since college. Angelica was at the end of her patience dealing with me too. Maybe I'd given her too many eye rolls and snide barbs to make her decidedly meager Deep Down pay worth it.

And now — Dante. Gone.

We'd known each other for a month. With his looks and fame, he could've had any man he wanted. Once word broke that Dante Huxley was gay — if word hadn't already broken — he was going to have every male homosexual this side of the Adriatic vying for him.

I was delusional to ever think he'd stay with me. Especially stay with me if I was going to be so fucking petulant. Me. With my dusty record store, my empty bank account, my prehistoric Range Rover, and my paint-thinner attitude? Dante could do so much better.

All I had going for me, if anything, were a fat cock, a quick mouth, and a cute cat. Maybe not in that order.

I'd forgotten how lucky, how rarified it was to have spent even a few weeks with Dante Huxley. How many other men, not to mention women, stayed up all night dreaming about it.

I lay back on my bed with eyes closed. That was the closest I could get to sleep. I knew I couldn't fall asleep. I didn't even set an alarm.

Morning broke. I desperately tried to catch at least an hour of sleep. I couldn't.

At seven thirty, I was up and out to Doctor Bryson's. The receptionist was waiting for me already. "You probably want to see your brave little girl, right?"

"Yes." I was nearly shaking — from lack of sleep, from the stress of Duchess in surgery, from knowing that this was the very event that had broken up me and Dante.

The receptionist opened the door to the presurgical room. I leaned down to Duchess and whispered in her ear. "You'll be fine." She smelled like medical disinfectant. Tubes ran to her mouth. I only hoped she didn't know that half of her coat was shaved off for the procedure.

"Hi, Mister Baker." The veterinarian shook my hand. "Duchess will be fine. But she's not going home today. You understand, right?"

"I understand." I sighed. I was ready for another uncomfortable night.

"Just wanted to make sure. There seems to be a whole entourage here for her." Doctor Bryson pointed in the direction of the waiting room.

"Entourage?"

"Your friend — the gentleman you told me not to contact — he's been here since opening."

"Oh." I exhaled and shook my head.

"We're getting ready to scrub in and start on Duchess's surgery." The vet made the universal gesture of shooing me out of the room. "So if you'll take your leave, please. We expect to have good news for you in an hour or so."

"Alright."

I stepped out to the waiting room. Dante stood there, holding a takeout bag from Penny's Pancakes.

I shook my head. I didn't need any of his bullshit.

He handed me the takeout breakfast bag. I took it, wordlessly, and went to the bathroom. I needed to at least splash water on my face before I went from dealing with my injured cat to dealing with my ex.

It had been — a night. I felt as if I'd been drinking coffee nonstop for the past twelve hours, even though I hadn't had a drop. I could barely feel the cold water on my face.

I hadn't even showered. And then I'd been touching Duchess. I needed a cleaning. I squirted soap into my cupped palms and washed my hands and face and even inside my congested nose. How many times I'd smirked when seeing people doing their morning hygiene in a public sink.

My nose cleared up. The Penny's Pancakes bag from Dante smelled exactly like a perfect breakfast over there: pancakes, toast, eggs, sausage. I could actually smell every part, even if I hadn't opened the box.

At least Dante had done that much for me.

I paper-toweled my face and walked back out to the waiting room to talk to him. Maybe we could at least — maybe he could at least give me his address to send his stuff to.

The waiting room was empty. "Dante?" He obviously wasn't in the bathroom I'd just come out of. I approached the reception desk.

"Have you seen—"

"Oh, he left a minute ago."

I sighed. Then I bolted. To the door. I could at least do something. I could at least talk to him.

Dante was standing just outside the clinic, clicking on his phone and squinting at approaching cars on the road. I must've looked like a madman, running up to him suddenly.

I pointed at Dante's phone. "Cancel that Uber!"

"Why?" He asked not like I was a stranger, but like I was the same old Ted — the same Ted who acted on the very borders of what people who cared about him would put up with.

"I'm sorry." I wanted to say so many things, but they all could've been summarized by this one thing. "I'm sorry I lashed out at you yesterday. I'm sorry I act like an asshole in general."

"It's understandable. I guess." Dante clicked through the screens to cancel his Uber request. "Your cat was injured. It was my fault. I was irritating you in general."

I held Dante's free hand in mine. "Understandable isn't excusable. I really need to stop that. Angelica warned me about this so many times. That my friends always allow me a next time, but one time, there won't be a next time."

Dante laughed. "Angelica should be the one writing song lyrics."

I sang to him. "'One time, there won't be a next time.' Sounds kind of like The Beatles, doesn't it?"

"Also sounds like a timely warning." Dante looked at me and sighed.

"I'm sorry. I really — I really need to change. I'll work on it. If you'll take me back. If you just give me a next time."

"I will, Ted." Dante leaned in and kissed my cheek.

I squeezed his hand again. Without saying anything, we walked back to Doctor Bryson's office. I opened the door for Dante. We walked in. The receptionist was busy checking in a family with a yapping brown Pomeranian.

Dante pointed over at the dog. "Dog looks like a cat."

I nodded in agreement. "That's a very cattish dog."

Dante shrugged. "Or a very doggish cat."

"Wise words." I nodded at Dante. We exchanged knowing, affectionate smiles. Just like old times — just like before the previous day's blow-up.

I lowered my voice and stepped closer to him, so close that my chest almost touched his shoulder. "Dante. I'm sorry if I never communicated it to you. But I missed you when you were gone, even just for yesterday evening. I couldn't sleep without you."

He whispered back to me: "I couldn't sleep without you either."

"I felt not right. Out of place. Missing something. Like a cattish dog." I smiled over at the Pomeranian and Dante burst out laughing.

"What's this about a cattish dog?" Doctor Bryson stood at our side. Dante and I simultaneously attempted to start to explain. She shook her head and waved that away. "I just came out here to say Duchess is out of surgery and she's doing great.

"Can we—" Dante started to ask. He took a small step toward the clinical area.

"No." The veterinarian shook her head as she spoke firmly. "No visitors. She got hit by a car yesterday, she got cut open today. She needs to sleep and rest. Give her a couple of days."

"At least I won't be completely lonely tonight," I blurted out while smiling at Dante.

The vet gave me an odd look, then a slightly uncomfortable smile. "Uh. Ok. None of my business, really." She quickly shook my hand, then Dante's, and disappeared behind a door.

I whispered to Dante: "Let's go home." I held up the Penny's Pancakes takeout bag, still untouched, still smelling like culinary orgasm.

We walked out to my car. By the time we reached the passenger door, my arm was around Dante's waist. His arm rested on my shoulder.

I started the car. Dante looked out the window. He was half-smiling.

I fished a cassette tape out of the center storage bin and popped it into the dashboard cassette player. It resoundingly clicked and pulled my tape inside.

"The tape player still works?" Dante smiled almost exuberantly.

"Sure does." I sighed. "I had the original restored. The restored British-made cassette player is probably worth more than the rest of the car."

"I love that vintage stuff. Tapes, cars, anything." Dante tapped his fingers on the center console. "Old anything."

"Guys?" I looked over and fluttered my eyebrows at Dante.

"You're not that old." He rolled his eyes.

"I'm from nineteen eighty-seven. Same year as this car. Heyday of cassette tapes. My parents named me after Ted Danson."

"Alright, that's old for a car. Not for a guy." Dante shook his head. "Hey, this song is 'Deep Down In Florida!'"

"Sure is. You know your stuff." I lightly tapped on the steering wheel as I steered through midday Honey Bay traffic.

"The album is called—" Dante squinted in thought, then suddenly remembered. "Isn't the album called—"

"*Hard Again*." I laughed. "The album is called *Hard Again*."

"And so am I!" Dante nodded.

"Ba da boom." I drummed on my steering wheel to acknowledge his joke. "Ba da boom, ba da bing."

Still sitting in his seat, Dante bowed to an imaginary audience. "Thank you. I'll be here all week."

"I hope so." I sighed. "Or maybe even longer than a week." I smiled at him as I parked my car in front of the house. The builders had pulled blue tarp over what had previously been Dante's room and there were vague sounds of hammers inside.

"I love being in Honey Bay. Even if I have to share a room with you." Dante smiled at me knowingly. "And I'm hard again."

"Hard *again*?" I laughed and shook my head. "You *are* young!" I opened his passenger-side door for him and held his hand as I led him inside, and upstairs.

"I can't control my physiology!" Dante theatrically gestured his innocence.

Inside my room, I kissed him: lips to lips, slowly, then our tongues pushing into each other's mouths. He pushed his body into mine. His dick pushed against my thigh.

"Did you mention something about being hard again?" I spoke down, directly into Dante's crotch. I unzipped his pants and pulled them down. His dick, perfectly hard and vertical inside his white briefs looked like a Grecian column.

I groped it just to make sure it was as rock-hard as it looked.

It was.

I looked up into Dante's eyes. "Can you lie down? I think we're both too exhausted to be standing up."

He stepped to the bed and stepped out of his pants and underwear. He lay back, wearing only a white shirt, and his long, hard dick pointing up at the ceiling.

I kissed his kneecap. He giggled. He giggled again when I kissed his other kneecap.

With my kisses I traced a line all the way up to his balls. I gave them a wet, slurpy suck.

I was too hungry for his dick to wait any longer. I breathed in the sweet smell of his precum. Deep inside: I opened wide and took the rock-hard, veiny shaft entirely into my mouth.

I sucked hard, like I wanted to suck all the conflict and uncertainty of our relationship out of him. All I could get was the honey-sweet syrup of his precum dripping onto my tongue. Maybe unlike me, Dante wasn't carrying bitterness, animosity, regret, and rancor around with him.

I bobbed my head up and down on his dick, letting it go all the way to my throat. Then I lifted his bare legs, so that he held them up in the air.

"Ah, Ted." Dante laughed and shook his head. "I'm a little too exhausted to get my ass pounded right now. Sorry."

"Yeah?" I kissed the underside of his thigh. "Good thing that's not what I'm about to do."

"I mean, as much as I love getting my ass pummeled." Dante laughed. "I had a long night."

"So did I." I sighed, aiming my warm breath at his sensitive dickhead. I laid my tongue at the top of his ass crack and slowly ran my tongue all the way to his taint. I ran a zigzag between the two sides of his asscrack.

"Oh fuck, man." Dante simultaneously laughed, shook, and moaned. He grabbed vaguely at my scalp and ran his hand through my hair. "I kind of forgot how good that felt."

"How quickly we forget!" I laughed right into his ass crack. I rolled up my tongue into a tongue-rod and teased his rim with it.

Dante grabbed his raised legs and thighs and spread them farther apart to give me more room.

I pushed my rolled-up tongue into his butthole, then pulled it out. I tongue-fucked Dante while he clenched his teeth and moaned pleasure.

Dante moaned. "Don't be selfish, man."

"This is selfish?" I fluttered my wet tongue up and down his rim.

"Extremely selfish." Dante moaned and pulled his knees closer to his shoulders to give me more room to eat his ass. "I wanna eat your ass too."

"That can be arranged." I made small love-nibbles up and down his rim, then sucked on his balls again. I popped his hard dick back into my mouth and sucked on it while I took off my shorts and underwear.

Dante's dick still deep in my mouth, I pushed his raised leg out of the way and rotated my body until my crotch straddled his face. When I dangled my cock, balls, taint, and ass over his face, Dante licked my dick like he was dying of acute penile deficiency. He slurped, licked, even gnawed up and down.

I blew on his dick to push it out of my mouth, then kissed his balls, and dove in again to eat his ass. His hole smelled like sweat and sex and I wanted all of it. I slurped on it, then put my lips to the whole and sucked on it. Dante's ass cheeks quivered.

"How's this?" Dante asked. He licked at the outer edge of my assrim.

I moaned in approval.

He licked deeper.

I moaned louder and lapped and slurped furiously in his ass while he was eating my ass. I tickled his rim with the tip of my pinkie finger.

He gasped, then moaned and pushed his crotch and ass harder against me. He pushed against my pinkie so hard that it looked like his tight, toned ass was going to swallow it.

I let my pinkie drift inside his butthole, and I circled my tongue while moaning and vibrating against his rim with my mouth.

Dante flicked his tongue up and down on my taint. "Mind if I raise the stakes a little?" He held his pointing finger up in the air, then licked it all over and sucked on it to lubricate it.

"I'm all for that." I separated my ass cheeks farther as I straddled his face.

His finger roamed in my ass: long and bony, slipping quickly in and moving around like he was drawing circles inside me.

I groaned hard.

He pushed his finger in and out, finger-fucking me.

I pushed my ass against him in rhythm with his finger. It felt like a thin, bony dildo. I clenched my ass muscles around his finger every time he was pulling out, just so I could feel every fold of his skin and every joint in his finger.

"Oh fuck." I moaned. He was finger-fucking me so hard that it started to hurt. "Slow down a little, man."

"Sorry, my bad." He slipped his finger out of me and looked at me from behind my thigh. "How's this instead?" He put his entire mouth to my rim, then licked my crack from bottom to top, then top to bottom, then back again.

"Oh my fucking God." My dick was involuntarily throbbing up against Dante's chin and chest.

He grabbed my dick and jerked it, while slurping and tongue-fucking my ass faster than before. "Hey Ted, are you gonna shoot your load on my chest while I eat your ass?" It sounded more like a demand than a question. He was jerking my dick harder and running his fingertips over the cocktip.

"Only if you return the favor, Dante." I kept licking his asshole and jerking his dick while I rubbed it all over my hairy chest.

Dante moaned. His ass cheeks tightened and clenched hard on my lips and tongue.

I jerked his dick harder. It throbbed. Ready.

Dante took over. He pushed his crotch hard into my hand. His dick shot hot cum on my chest.

I kept jerking it.

Another rope coated my pecs. I aimed his dick to put the third shot on my stomach while I kept licking inside his clenched ass.

"Oh fuck." Dante's voice was down to a whisper. He did exactly the same for me as I'd done for him. His tongue and lips went deep into my hole. He drew circles with his tongue inside my ass. He jerked my dick while running the cocktip all over his tight chest.

When my cocktip ran over Dante's pecs, I couldn't restrain my orgasm. The shuddering climax rose up from deep inside of me — my legs shaking—and exploded out in ropes of cum. I grabbed hard onto Dante's dick and his leg as I shook and came on his chest.

He pumped out every drop of my cum. The smell of my cum filled the room.

"Mmm, tasty." I craned my neck to see Dante sucking on his finger and smiling at me. "Sweet and delicious, and you haven't even eaten the French toast I brought you."

I swiped my hand across my chest. It reeked of Dante's cum. I licked it and smiled at him just as he'd smiled at me. "Yours is delicious too."

My phone rang in my pocket. It was the tone I had reserved for calls from Deep Down.

Unromantically, I quickly licked and wiped the cum off my hand, then got up off Dante and picked up my phone from the floor.

"Ted, you ok?" Angelica had reason to be worried: I'd never, in my ten years of running Deep Down Music, been absent at work unannounced.

"Better than ok." I laughed. "I'm taking the day off. The shop's all yours. Don't go crazy."

"Things going well with Daaaaante?" Angelica drew out his name, like a schoolyard taunt. She knew me all too well.

"None of your business and yes and bye-bye." I laughed as I clicked off the phone and laid it back on the nightstand. I took the takeout bag from Penny's Pancakes and brought it to bed. I sat next to Dante and sniffed inside the bag.

"What did they say about not eating crackers in bed?" Dante wagged a finger at me, his eyes still on the takeout bag.

"They didn't mention French toast." I opened the plastic wrap, then the styrofoam box inside. A half-day old, it still smelled great. The smell was perfect for our sunny bedroom that already smelled like sweat and sex. I sighed and nodded at Dante. "You know, Dante, French toast is like a rimjob."

"Even when it's bad, it's good?" Dante snapped his fingers in the air.

"Exactly!" I awkwardly high-fived Dante from my seat next to him. Maybe my misdeeds of the past day — of my life, actually — had been forgiven, if not forgotten. "Just like a rimjob."

With one hand I put a piece of French toast in Dante's mouth. With my other hand I put a piece in my own mouth.

"What kind of a heathen doesn't add butter and syrup?" Dante looked at me cockeyed.

"Check this out. This is how we ate French toast at NYU." I lay my head back and opened my mouth wide. Then I squeezed from the syrup and butter containers directly onto the French toast inside my mouth.

"What the actual fuck?" Dante shook his head. "Have you never heard of plates?"

"We used to get French toast from this street takeout counter." I was laughing while recounting it. "Great French toast. Three bucks. No plates, no nothing. Communal syrup and butter, at the counter."

"Eww." Dante winced. "Don't need more details."

"And straight people think rimjobs are disgusting, right?" I laughed.

"I've never cum so hard in my life." Dante sighed. "It's like at twenty-two years old I'm finally discovering sex."

"I'm thirty-two and kind of feeling the same way." I shrugged. "I mean it's certainly not my first time, you know, but it's never felt nearly like this."

I chewed on my syruped and buttered French toast then leaned in to kiss Dante. As we kissed, I used my tongue to transfer some half-chewed French toast to his mouth. He chewed it while looking at me with faux disgust.

"Am I a fucking baby bird?" Dante laughed. He moved his arms like wings at his sides. "Little birdie getting fed French toast in bed?"

"Maybe."

"I'd complain that eating out of your mouth is fucking gross." Dante shook his head while still chewing. "I would, if I weren't so fucking hungry. I still have two songs to write, by the way."

"That's cool." I shrugged. "I need to catch up on sleep. And I'll finish whatever portion of that French toast you're not gonna eat."

Dante shook his head. "First you eat my ass, then my French toast?"

"What can I say." I leaned in and kissed his cheek. "I enjoy the finer things."

14

Dante

"**A**nother one!" I tore the paper out of the notebook and threw my pencil at the wall. Hard. The frustration of wasted hours was messing with my usual calm.

I was behaving like Ted, a little, but I couldn't control it. Maybe he couldn't control it either.

"Another what?" Ted popped his head out from under his comforter. "I thought it was the roof repair guys making noise, but it's already night."

"Another verse I was trying to write that didn't turn out right." I drummed on Ted's desk with two pens at once. "Now I know how you feel when you get frustrated."

"Don't be like me, man." Ted groaned, like groaning in dissatisfaction at himself. "Ain't nobody who likes a guy who lashes out like that."

"I know." I sighed. "Just that I've been sitting here at your desk for hours, staring at this notebook and this screen, and I can't come up with anything." I twirled my pen around my fingers.

"I thought the kitchen was your workspace." Ted had his fluffy white comforter pulled up so it reached his mouth. It resembled a huge milk mustache.

"Feels better being near you." I smiled. "Cheesy but true."

"Feels better being near you, when I'm right there with my boo. Never want to be far, even when I'm a star." Ted shrugged as he sang the lyrics. "How's that?"

"Holy shit. Holy shit again." I shook my head at him. What he'd come up with was a lot better than I'd managed to come up with all afternoon. "That's cheesy, it's at least something. You're brilliant."

"No, I'm definitely not. But I can try to help you out."

"Those lines are good though. Better than the crap I came up with after staring at this all day." I waved my notebook at him and pointed at my screensaver-displaying laptop. "You're a professional. Or— you're almost as good as a professional." I tempered down my words, so as not to send him into a rage again.

"You want to know the story?" Ted spoke into his comforter. "I can tell you the story. The story behind my obvious complex."

"I do. I want to know all your stories, Ted. All your stories and your fears and your complexes. This one, I've been afraid to ask about."

"Here goes." He pulled the comforter down from his mouth. "I wanted to be a professional songwriter and music producer." Ted sighed. "I studied music composition and songwriting at NYU. Came back here, started the music store, then left Angelica to run it while I went back to New York to try to make it in songwriting."

"You were dreaming of becoming the toast of the Brill Building?" I laughed. Everyone in the business knew the Brill Building.

"Holy shit, how did you know — oh yeah, you're actually in the music industry." Ted shook his head. "The record companies aren't actually in the Brill Building anymore, of course. But yeah, I was hustling around NYC. Driving fucking Uber to pay the bills while I pitched my songs around all five fucking boroughs."

"You? Driving Uber?" Somehow that made me laugh. "I only imagine you as the naked guy in the window yelling at my Uber limo."

"Well now you know."

"So what happened? I mean with your songwriting career?"

"I put all my effort into it, Dante. I really did. I studied, I practiced, I memorized. I used a whole month of Uber pay to buy Avid Pro Tools."

"So that's how you know about Pro Tools." I gave him a thumbs-up. Avid Pro Tools was a bit of knowledge that usually separated music industry insiders from mere fans.

"Yeah, that's how I know about Pro Tools. And that's how I know about taking my songs to so many record companies, artists, producers, conventions, meetups, exhibitions, blah blah."

"And what happened?" I went to bed and lay face up next to him, my left arm on top of his right arm.

"Well." Ted took a deep breath and looked outside the window into the night, like he was trying to catch a tiny glimpse of the ocean between the trees. "The few producers who actually let me pitch to them told me that my music was—" Ted cleared his throat and looked at me. "Can you guess?"

"Too esoteric, too elite, too highbrow?" It was all I could think of for Ted's tastes.

"Nah." He smiled wryly. "Too poppy. They said it's pop garbage and not serious music. Lacks gravitas. Bubblegum pop."

"Oh shit." My stomach sank on Ted's behalf. I couldn't even begin to imagine how much that must've hurt him. "Your music? Too poppy?"

"I know, I know." Ted bit his lip. "So you know. That's why I've got a sore spot now. A bit."

"Just a tiny bit." I turned to my side, kissed his forehead, and stretched my arm over his chest. "That's all in the past though. And right now you can live your dream, right?"

"Having a boyfriend like you, you mean?"

"Ok, maybe." I squeezed him closer. "But I mean writing some lyrics. We can write lyrics together for the concert. You can even go over and fix some of the stuff I already wrote."

"That is living my dream actually."

"Yeah. The Brill Building right in your bedroom, you know?" I got up, took my notebook, pens and pencils, and my laptop, and brought it all back to bed. "We can do the writing here. Together."

"What if we get tired of writing songs?" There was that knowing, naughty grin on Ted's face. "Are there other activities we could partake of in bed?"

"Sure." I shrugged. "I'm sure writing songs isn't the only skill you learned in New York."

"Who told you?" Ted's face screamed wide-eyed shock.

"A little birdie." I flapped my arm-wings again. "A little birdie who eats pre-chewed French toast."

"Well the other thing I learned in New York." Ted looked up at the ceiling for a second, then out the window. "Is that sex isn't all that much fun if you're just hooking up with strangers. Never had it better than with you, right here."

I whispered in Ted's ear: "That rimjob was even better than French toast."

15

Ted

I hadn't even seen that rhinestone-glitter shirt in Dante's wardrobe. He certainly never wore it around the house. But he was always my rock star at home, even without a rhinestone shirt.

Now, up on stage, jeweled shirt and all, he was a perfect pop idol: Justin Bieber without the trashiness, or One Direction without the cluelessness. I had to snap myself into reality to remember that *yes* this was my boyfriend, *no* I wasn't dreaming.

From the front row, my viewing angle of Dante was the same as when I sucked his dick at home. Except now, he was wearing pants.

He was tuning his guitar, adjusting the amplifiers, and chatting with the backup band Baxter and Andy had hired for him.

"You're Ted?" A big, burly dude with a just-fuck-my-shit-up haircut put his hand out to me. He looked just like every music industry insider who'd crushed my ego back in New York.

"I sure am." I shook his hand.

"I'm Justice Worthington. Dante's manager."

"Ah, ok. Great." I restrained myself from voicing musicians' usual complaints about parasitic managers.

"Dante says you wrote most of his new songs for him."

"Ah—" I shook my head and waved my hand. It was better not to get into that.

Up on stage, Dante got that precarious, frightened look. His face was paler than usual. His eyes scanned the front of the audience.

"Go Dante!" I shouted up at him.

He noticed me in the front row. His facial expression relaxed. He gave me a thumbs-up and adjusted his guitar again.

He came to life on stage. "Hello, Honey Bay!" His voice boomed from the speakers propped up all over the makeshift outdoor arena. "I'm here to sing some songs, fund an animal shelter, and hang out with all of you for an hour or two."

The crowd replied with scream-roar-applause.

I'd been avoiding looking at the crowds behind me. With that much noise, I had to look back now. Not that many people turned out in Honey Bay for anything. They could've been handing out free French toast at Penny's and we wouldn't have gotten a crowd like that.

Dante's manager, Justice, tapped my shoulder. "People flew in from all over the country." The industrial-strength mint on his breath was strong enough to make me woozy.

Dante cleared his throat on stage. "My first song tonight. A bit of a simple rhythm-guitar ditty. It's called 'My Cat Isn't Fat.'"

I laughed. We'd co-written that one only the previous evening, while reminiscing about our first meeting.

Justice Worthington tapped my shoulder again. "One of your songs, right?"

"I guess." I shrugged. Maybe I could practice trying to be modest. For once.

"You really should consider a career—" Justice was almost screaming into my ear. I was the one being pitched, for a change. I pointed up at Dante on the stage. I was there to support him, not network for my own potential songwriting career.

Dante started into the song, smiling directly at me the whole time. We'd just thrown it together quickly: garage rock with a bass guitar and simple lyrics, almost like the Ramones or something.

At a pause in the guitar section, Dante pointed into the audience and made a double thumbs-up. I looked over and had to laugh. Andy and Baxter were waving glow sticks in rhythm with the song. They looked every bit the former high school sweethearts they were.

"Next up!" Dante spoke into the microphone. The crowd quieted and listened, enraptured. "Next up is a song from my old band, Inferno. I'm not with Inferno anymore, but we made some pretty good music. And I still get royalties, so go buy our album." The crowd laughed. "I knew Inferno really hit it big when our albums showed up at Deep Down Music in Honey Bay." More crowd laughter.

Dante went right into the song. There was no bitterness there. He sang both his and Roland's parts without a hitch.

At the end of the song, he gulped from a bottle of water and spoke into the microphone again. "I hold no ill will toward Inferno, by the way. Since I'm still getting royalties." Laughter again. "No, seriously. I'm sure you guys have heard the story a million times. But what you might not know is the breakup of Inferno and the breakup of my relationship with Kate led me to find out who I really am."

Dante paused and looked around. The audience was hanging on his next word.

"I'm a singer-songwriter. Well, more of a singer, really. I need some help with the songwriting." The audience laughed. "And I'm a gay man. If you don't know, well now you know." Dante laughed. Some applause came from the audience, along with some shocked looks.

"And along those lines, the next song I've got for you is called 'This Love Is No Wheelbarrow.' A very special man in my life helped me write it. Or actually, he wrote most of it; lawyers please take note for once the royalty checks start coming in."

Dante launched into that dumb, silly song, quietly smiling down at me in the first row.

"Ted!" I turned around to see Baxter. He threw me two neon-green glow sticks. I yelled a thank-you to him as best I could and swayed to the music, glow sticks and all.

What was supposed to be a ninety-minute concert went for a whole three hours. Dante looked, and played, better than I'd ever seen.

The last song — the second encore — was "One Time There Won't Be A Next Time." Dante was singing it, but that was my lesson to learn.

After the applause died down, Dante spoke into the microphone again. "I'd love to sing more for you guys, but I don't want to tire out the band." He laughed. "There will indeed be a next time. And I will indeed be in Honey Bay."

Dante hopped down from the stage to the area between the stage and the front row. He held a hand out to me and drew me closer to him.

We kissed: his hot, dry lips, his matted hair, his flushed-red face, sweat rolling down his forehead, his guitar still hanging from his neck.

"Dude." Dante shook his head. "I played better up there than I ever did before. It was like I had a rock and roll demon in me." He laughed.

"Must be the guitar?" I asked. "Or the rhinestone shirt?"

"Or you being right here and supporting me." He kissed me again. It felt like the lights of a thousand phones were on us. They probably were. People were definitely filming. Reporters were definitely pointing their big phallic lenses at us.

"Dante Huxley!" One grungy looking reporter made his way through the crowd. "I'm Jack Falls with *Rolling Stone*. Great show! Amazing show! You rocked it out of the park."

"Thanks." Dante nodded politely.

"I know what happened between you and Kate." The reporter stared at Dante like he wanted some kind of confirmation.

"You'd better know." Dante laughed. "You guys did a cover story on it."

"Oh. Right." The reporter looked like he'd just been told to sit down. He stepped back a little. "I wanted to ask you, is this gentleman with you your boyfriend?" The reporter stuck his phone's microphone toward Dante's face.

"He is." Dante wrapped his arm around me. "Songwriter and boyfriend. Best friend. Lover. Also landlord."

"Quite a list!" The reporter said into his phone's microphone, then held it in front of Dante's mouth again. "Would you say he's the secret of your success?"

"Sort of. But he's no secret now." Dante smiled at me and at the reporter, then subtly shooed him away. He perfunctorily answered a few other questions from a few other reporters and fans, but after three hours of playing, I wanted to take him home to rest. He perfectly understood my top-secret hand signals and we made our way out.

Back home, I led Dante directly to bed.

My songwriting professors back in school who'd always said that performers did the easy part didn't know shit. Dante looked like a miner who'd just come up for air. He collapsed into bed and fell asleep face-first, without even rolling over.

I lay on my side next to him and slowly fell asleep, inhaling his sweaty, tired smell. I didn't even attempt to wake him the following morning. I tiptoed out to work while Dante seemed to be in the midst of some deep REM sleep, even at nine in the morning.

Angelica greeted me at the very front door. "That was awesome!"

"What was awesome?" I smiled. It was my usual act-stupid bit for her.

"The sex you guys had after the concert last night." Angelica nodded confidently. "It must've been awesome."

"Bzzt, wrong!" I clapped my hands in front of her face. "We were both too tired! We went right to sleep!"

"Alright." Angelica's face conceded defeat. "The concert was awesome. And I just heard on *Andy In The A.M.* how much money it raised."

"How much?" I was cautiously optimistic.

"Well, out of a hundred thousand goal, right?" Angelica stepped to the whiteboard on the wall and wrote *$100,000*.

"Yeah."

"Out of a hundred thousand goal." Angelica blew on the tip of the marker. "We raised two hundred five thousand, one hundred thirty-seven dollars." She wrote $205,137 on the same whiteboard.

"So what does that mean?" I tapped on the whiteboard. "Alice Silver is up to her tits in coke and hookers?"

"Stop!" Angelica grimaced. "Alice Silver is a nice lady."

"I know that. That's why I make fun of her."

"Ok, ok." Angelica shook her head. "Anyway, it means that in addition to rebuilding the shelter, we can actually expand it, and have a few months' operating budget in store."

"I'm hoping." I spoke to Angelica quietly. "I'm hoping Dante can do more Honey Bay benefit concerts like that in the future."

"He's staying in Honey Bay?" Angelica looked at me.

"I'm in Honey Bay, right?"

"But—" Angelica looked down at the floor. "Right." She ran off to a shelf and started straightening some CDs.

"Hey Angelica, I'm taking the rest of today off too. Gotta pick up Duchess from the vet."

"Yeah, how's Duchess?"

"Doing great. Ready to go home. I'll have Dante sing 'My Cat Isn't Fat' to her."

"Awesome!" Angelica nodded.

"If Dante hasn't already run away from me as you think he will." I shook my head at her and stepped outside to my car before she could reply.

At the clinic, Doctor Bryson was standing in front of the reception desk. "Amazing concert!"

"You were there?"

"Is that a short-people joke?" She made a faux-angry face at me and held her palm above her head. She was five feet tall, max.

"No. I just didn't see you."

"You're just making it worse." She laughed. "Just teasing you though. We were way back in the cheap seats. And we saw you and Dante, and it was amazing."

"Great. Great you enjoyed it."

"And your cat, who isn't fat by the way, is ready to go home." Doctor Bryson walked me back to the room where Duchess sat in a kennel. She put her hand through the door and patted Duchess's belly. "She's not fat, just, a bit, you know—"

"Zaftig," I said. "*Zaftig* is the term."

"Exactly." Doctor Bryson covered her laugh and let Duchess hop from the holding kennel into her carrier. "So that was actually Dante Huxley that was here with you the other day?"

"Yup." I lifted the carrier so I could look at Duchess face-to-face, then set her down on the table while I talked with the vet.

"I thought your hoodie-wearing friend looked like someone famous. I didn't want to say anything. Part of Duchess's entourage, you know."

"She brings all the celebrities to the house." I tapped on Duchess's carrier.

"That's awesome that Dante Huxley happened to be in Honey Bay when we needed to do a fundraiser for the shelter."

"Dante will be staying here in Honey Bay."

"Dante Huxley?" The vet shook her head.

"You heard at the concert, right? He's my boyfriend."

"And he'll be staying here?" Doctor Bryson spoke as if she were playing along with a fantasy. "Dante Huxley will be living here with you in Honey Bay?"

"Sure, why not?"

"Alright." Doctor Bryson shrugged. "If you say so." She shook her head and walked back into her clinical area without saying goodbye. I took Duchess in her carrier, buckled it into the front seat of my car, and drove home.

Was I the stupid one, thinking Dante was really going to stick around?

I parked in front of the house, walked in, and gently set Duchess on her favorite sitting spot on the sofa.

Dante walked into the living room, naked, singing to himself.

"Holy shit, you're bright-eyed and bushy-tailed!" I laughed.

"I've already got a new song half-written. I figure I can have enough material for a whole album by next month. I already talked to Justice about it."

"And then what?" I asked.

"What do you mean *and then what*?" Dante sang some lines while waving his arms and shaking his dangling cock. "And then I embark on my solo career."

"Oh, I see." I looked out the window.

"What? Is something wrong?"

"I'm just realizing that I'm just a pit stop here on your career. You'll go off on your solo career, your new life, and it's all over for me. I'll just be a momentary diversion you had when you needed one."

"What? Ted. Can't you feel how I feel about you?"

"I'm used to it. Just like Angelica says: people I care about will leave me. So thanks for warning me in advance about your career. Or any other excuses you can come up with for walking out of here." I turned my back to Dante so he wouldn't see my eyes water.

"Ted. I know where this is coming from."

"Where what is coming from?" I felt my face flush red. Of course, I also knew where it was coming from.

"Ted. I know. You're afraid of being abandoned by me. I won't abandon you."

"Really, seriously?" I turned around to face him.

"Really, seriously, Ted." He wrapped his arms around my back. "News flash: I love you. I need you. I've never been as happy as I am with you."

"So it's not just rebound sex after you broke up with Kate, finding some random fan to stick your dick into while you wait for someone worthy to come along?"

"Ted, you weren't even my fan! You probably still aren't!"

I had to break out laughing. "Ok, I wasn't. I am now though."

"Really?"

"Yes, really, I'm your fan." I kissed his lips and slipped my tongue inside his mouth. I ran my hands up and down his tight, toned back and ass. "So touring is not a way to run away from me?"

"Good God, Ted." Dante laughed. "It's not. I can tour while still visiting you. Or you can come visit me on tour. And I'm not going to be touring all the time, you know. I'm not the fucking Grateful Dead."

I laughed again. "I wouldn't be particularly eager to give The Grateful Dead a rimjob."

"You know what they say about rimjobs, though." Dante pointed two fingers at me.

"Yeah, yeah. That a rimjob from a grumpy, ill-tempered guy is better than no rimjob at all?" I smiled at him.

"Almost right." Dante whispered in my ear. "That a rimjob from the grumpy, ill-tempered man I love is better than any other rimjob at all."

Epilogue

Dante

"Those kids. Davie and Dakota. The two little girls. They were adorable." Justice sighed as we rode home from the re-opening of the new and expanded animal shelter.

"Yeah, those little girls were the first to pitch the idea to me." I tapped on the window glass. "Those two little girls kind of restarted my career."

"Social entrepreneurs, they are." Ted nodded. "Hope of the future." He pulled up in front of the house. The same construction workers who'd fixed up my former room into our new guest bedroom had also installed a fully screened-in second patio just for Duchess to hang out in.

I led the three of us in through the entrance to Duchess's new patio. My royalties had paid for it, so I had reason to be proud.

Justice smiled and looked around. "You've got — you've got like a screened, semi-outdoor playroom for your cat?"

"Sure do." I gave Justice a thumbs-up. "Quite a bit cheaper to have that here than in Manhattan." Justice measured the room, holding up his fingers to his eyes. "I think this screened patio is bigger than my entire Manhattan apartment."

"Well, Duchess deserves it." I squatted down and petted Duchess. Her surgical scars were almost invisible after three months of recovery. "She's a good girl, and she's just finished healing from surgery."

"This screened patio is called a Florida room." Ted held Duchess up to his face. "Duchess, did you even know that it's called a Florida room? Did you even know it's all for you, pretty girl?"

CHERISH HIM

"The first monthly payout on 'My Cat Isn't Fat' paid for that," I said to Justice. "I figured I'd use some of the money to make her happy. And keep her safe."

"So the song is about her?" Justice asked.

"Hey, now." I clicked my tongue. "*Our* cat isn't fat."

"Did you hear that, Duchess?" Ted looked at Duchess and petted her with his toe. "You're not fat. And you're not just mine but *ours*. Or Dante and I are *yours*. Or something like that."

I picked up Duchess and rubbed my nose against hers, then handed her to Ted to hold again. "I actually offered to donate some of the song money to the animal shelter, but they said after the concert they've got more cash than they can use."

"Dante, as your manager, I am well aware of your song's number-three position on the charts, and the quite generous checks that we all just received." Justice held up a gargantuan watch on his wrist. "This may come as a surprise, but I've also been enjoying the fruits of our labors."

"Is that a Patek Philippe?" Ted squinted at Justice's watch, then let Duchess look at it.

"No, it's my big hairy arm." Justice laughed and flexed his arm at Ted. "Yes, it's a Patek Philippe. Impressive that you know. Most people think it's a Rolex."

"Rolex?" Ted rolled his eyes. "That's for used car salesmen and Amway tycoons." He shook his head in disgust.

"Ted is a real connoisseur, a bon vivant." I took a swig of beer. "Enjoys all the finer things. Exquisite sense of taste. Even listens to old Inferno CDs." I massaged Ted's shoulders.

"Are you trying to give me a hernia?" Ted looked back over his shoulder with faux annoyance.

"No, but you almost gave me one last night." I giggled.

Justice cringed and shook his head. "Um, I hate to be a Dutch uncle here, guys." He was tapping at something on his tablet. "But we have to keep the money coming in if we don't want to end up like MC Hammer."

"Can't touch this." Ted snapped two fingers in the air.

"Yeah, we *don't* want to be like that guy." Justice laughed. "So I've got a proposed tour schedule for Dante here, to keep the money coming. Album sales don't make much money nowadays."

"How long am I not going to be able to see Dante?" Ted's voice suddenly turned serious.

"Ah. Dante already gave me the specifications on that." Justice swiped through his tablet and showed Ted the email I'd sent him. "See? Dante demands to have at least seventy-two hours in Honey Bay every two weeks. And see what he wrote? 'Because he really isn't himself without you.' And see what else he wrote? 'Because he loves you.'"

Ted nodded. "Yeah, as expected. Everybody always wants to be near me."

I squeezed Ted's ass cheek.

"Alright, correction." Ted took a swig of beer and looked out at the sunset in the distance. "My beloved Dante always wants to be near me."

Dante nodded at me. "Because you're such a big pop star sensation."

I rolled my eyes in response, then kissed him, hard.

Also by Steve Milton

Badboy Gay Mafia
Love and Zika
The Sticky Icky
Swimming to Cuba

College Try
Winter Break
Summer Project
Back to School
Student Health
College Try

Collins Avenue Confidential
The Mechanic and the Surgeon
Swing State
The Minister and the Rock Star
Judging Valentine
High School Reunion
The Big Comeback
The Pilot and the Professor

Dreamboat Island
Crema
Landing Love
Meow
Pretend Like You Mean It
And Then Everything Changed

Gay Getaways
Ex on the Beach

Honey Bay
Remember Him
Cherish Him
Embrace Him
Rescue Him
It Wasn't Supposed to Happen

Love Against The Odds
Civil Wars

Straight Guys
Call It What You Want
Straight Guys: Eleven Gay Romance Novellas

Three Straight
We Three
Three Hearts
The Law of Three
When We're Together: MMM Gay Romance Collection

Standalone
The Power of Three

About the Author

Steve Milton writes sexy, snarky feel-good stories about men loving men. Expect lots of laughs and not much angst.

Steve's most recent series is Gay Getaways.

He is a South Florida native, and when he's not writing, he likes cats, cars, music, and coffee.

Sign up for Steve's monthly updates: http://eepurl.com/bYQboP

He is happy to correspond with his readers by email. Email stevemiltonbooks@gmail.com

Lightning Source UK Ltd.
Milton Keynes UK
UKHW040800060323
418105UK00001B/263